Max's passion for literature bloomed when he was young. He recounts his earliest memories reading *1984* and *War of the Worlds,* sparking an everlasting love for literature, as if their dystopian worlds seemed more hopeful than our own. The macabre side of literature and film is where his preferences lie. First and foremost, his love for these arts derived from a lifelong fascination with narratives and their power to transport you elsewhere, leave troublesome worries aside, and enter a realm of imaginative self-indulgence.

Max Michael Wightwick

A Bigot's Guide to Salvation

AUSTIN MACAULEY PUBLISHERS™
LONDON · CAMBRIDGE · NEW YORK · SHARJAH

Copyright © Max Michael Wightwick 2024

The right of Max Michael Wightwick to be identified as author of this work has been asserted by the author in accordance with sections 77 and 78 of the Copyright, Designs and Patents Act 1988.

All rights reserved. No part of this publication may be reproduced, stored in a retrieval system, or transmitted in any form or by any means, electronic, mechanical, photocopying, recording, or otherwise, without the prior permission of the publishers.

Any person who commits any unauthorised act in relation to this publication may be liable to criminal prosecution and civil claims for damages.

This is a work of fiction. Names, characters, businesses, places, events, locales, and incidents are either the products of the author's imagination or used in a fictitious manner. Any resemblance to actual persons, living or dead, or actual events is purely coincidental.

A CIP catalogue record for this title is available from the British Library.

ISBN 9781035844173 (Paperback)
ISBN 9781035844180 (ePub e-book)

www.austinmacauley.com

First Published 2024
Austin Macauley Publishers Ltd®
1 Canada Square
Canary Wharf
London
E14 5AA

I would like to thank Austin Macauley Publishers for their appreciation and confidence in me. I would similarly like to thank my grandmother for propelling my inward faith, allowing me to believe in my writing.

Table of content

A Bigot's Guide to Salvation — 11

A Wishful Artist — 12

Trigger Happy — 20

A Needle in a Haystack — 32

Face to Face — 36

You May Now Kiss the Mistress — 70

The Three Stages of Grief — 81

The Man from Mars — 120

Nurture Over Nature — 130

The Dance of the Suicidal Faun — 164

The Changeling — 183

The Fisherman's Catch — 196

Epilogue — 205

A Bigot's Guide to Salvation

When all thou sows are sinful performances, thou shalt reap divine punishment.

A Wishful Artist

There comes a point in any miserable being's life where a crisis sets in. Fame and money all come with a price. You sell your authenticity for cheap thrills. Money pays the bills, but what truly quenches the ill desires? This artist, Ted Hughes, was an intellectual. He had a period where his art was regarded as perfect. His work was marvelled at, and every child was taught to dissect his perfect work. Nevertheless, when one is propped up on a golden pedestal filled with ancient jewels, it becomes thick with slippery ice. With one wrong slice, you can slip into oblivion. I would be lying if I said to you that you could get much higher. It becomes dire after a while. You become that ancient jewel shoved away in some forgotten shopping aisle. So, ride the Nile and follow it to the end of the nocturne.

The engraving by Ted Hughes had become a worn-out ornament. It had become Pablo Picasso, a commercialised rêve sold on a silver platter. His work force fed on every trite market table. Hughes' was a dove who no longer descended upon lovers. He was no symbol of freedom, or a servant of peace. Women wept at his ineptitude. They slept at the thought of him. Mammy swept his paintings under the sofa, hoping her master would not upbraid her for leaving them out too long. Ted sat puzzled, troubled, and perplexed at how he had let his fame shame him. He sat by his amber whiskey, humming the tune of Alabama's prehistoric national anthem. O' don't ask why! The door stared him right in the glaucous eye. His glass whispered, loathing him for becoming a fly on a wall. Why don't you just die? said a shadowy scourge. All he heard were the school bullies deriding his worth. He refilled his crystal ship and drank from it. Each sip sinking him deeper into unconsciousness. Each sip broke him through to the other side. The forbidden fruit lay his arse bare; on occasion, letting out an unruly snare. Suddenly the phone rang. It had a queer tang to it. He begrudgingly picked her up, and placed her to his blocked ear. No one bothered to ring nowadays. It left him with a bitter sting, a tight G-string between his crotches. A voice spoke so gently and kindly, that he had forgotten people could be affable.

"Hughes, look, Brother, we need this project finished soon. We gave you the canvas, studio - everything you need," hoarsening their voice, "Will you be able to finish her within a week?" It sounded so caring and so sincere. His alcohol-ridden breath seeped through the landline, like a salty brine.

"Michael, I physically can't; my mind bends and ends with the same conclusion. Nothing seems to work. Even liquor has disowned me." Hughes mewled his pity.

"Look, you have your duties; I got you this fucking job; don't be a yob. Make anything Hughes - anything. Paint a fucking rose, a self-portrait - SOMETHING I BEG OF YOU!" a desperate taciturnity besought Hughes, and then, the line went dumb. His last friend had forsaken him. Hughes' anger grew fat, and impregnated with a righteous self-importance.

Who did Michael think he was? Why doesn't he try so hard, if it really is that simple?

Hughes stood up and wandered to his blank, emotionless canvas. He had turned her the other way, so as to avoid her reprove: it reminded him of his beloved mother. They never got along; she always dug her nails in him. Hammering, hammering, building resentment into him, as she had likewise done to their father. Who, inevitably, did the honourable thing and took his own life due to these harrying circumstances. What was Hughes to paint? He had no faint idea. A saint? O' how quaint! No, he needed something rife with emotions.

Five minutes had passed by now, and nothing came from his mind. Was he really so purblind? His third eye, a once all seeing, all-knowing mind, had become but blind. The canvas stared at him, cursing, just like his mother used to. He downed his glass of whiskey, and threw it at the wall. Stand tall, don't let her lowball you. He wrought to empower himself, feel something besides abashment, alas, he could not do so, with the serpentine scorn of his mother in his ear. He was always a slave to his mother's temper. In a rueful instant, his legs broke, crashing to the floor. He wept, his childhood trauma crept, knocking on Present's door.

God impromptu shone a brilliant light. It gave him a jolly good fright, for at last, he knew what was wrong. His vision, and eyes, had been deceiving him. They were holding him back. Preventing the true Einstein from being unleashed upon the idiotic world. If only he could eviscerate them from their gorges, his whole existence would be whirled into a novel kind of productivity. He raised his hands to the sky, and with all the pity left within him, he cried out, "O lord, if you hear me, with your finest tweezers, pluck out my eyes! Clear me of my useless sight. Let it cause me great spite! All I plead for is a need of sightless clarity! Think of the endless possibilities." Tears flooded from his wobegone face. He, after much prayerful vanity, decided it was now time to slumber. There was, after all, no God. No big man is watching from hidden in the empyrean above. That had just been one sick game to control the peasants in the mediaeval ages. Tomorrow is but a day away, thought Hughes. Another lonesome day for him to keep his daemons at bay.

He lifted his sterile, anaemia-white duvet open. She let him inside. He, after all, needed a place to reside. His mother never comforted him at night, never joined him in bed, and lent a shoulder to cry upon. Here, in this homely bed, he sought an easeful connection. He hefted his arthritic thumb, placed it betwixt his two front teeth, and heaved. His thumb was constricted under such enormous pressure, nevertheless, it was his way of cosseting himself. His last thoughts, before he drifted into paralytic insomnolence, were of the morrow. He had to deliver something, lest he wished to dissolve amongst irrelevancies alike. Being the lauded Ted Hughes, though, he was inoculated against these strains of ailments - or so he believed.

The birds burped their ungentlemanly songs, waking him from his inert sopor. There was an awkward cumber, blockading his eyes from opening. The room seemed so dark, and yet it was April. The Berlin Wall seemed to have been built during his rest, commanded by doltish Trump. Had Hughes himself contracted some overnight lurgy? Had a non-self-organism initiated war? He pried his lids ajar, however, no light passed through, he saw but a thick gloaming. His pupils were vacant to anything save the colour black. An onyx would have been brighter than what he saw. His jaw was in awe. Saliva drooled down his pores and neck. The Three Gorges gave way to copious amounts of sweat. London Bridge was to fall. His head began pounding with a megrim. He hankered for paracetamol. But how was he to find this remedy in the ocean of shades before him? A tsunami of guilt rushed his nervous system. He recalled his damnatory wish.

Alas, how many times had he asked and supplicated the aid from an angel in heaven, and been given no such avail?!

He must have summoned Lucifer, for this was he who was to suffer. He had become an artistic martyr. His mind had been reduced to a Windows XP buffer.

His fear began to subside, it soon became his newly-wedded bride. What does a blind man feel? Do they suffer from their own prejudices? The white man's burden. One man's pride is another man's prejudice. The black man deals with racism, the female is handed misogyny, but what did the blind man face? Was he his own, individual race? All these toilsome notions were injected into Hughes' cell membrane. He was coming to terms with the life beggared in his fore.

Light started to glisten, as he shivered inside his carapace. He removed his cancerous self-contempt from where it resided, and handed it an eviction slip. He bit his lip, haemorrhaging blood. The metallic taste poured over his feverous senses. Images flashed within his erratic mind. He saw colours; these colours had no real form, all the same, they caused a swarm of philosophical thoughts to brew. Thunder fulgurated, and struck him. Paintings inundated his imagination: olde mosaics, ruined temples, otherworldly images. Lisas moaning and shouting at their husbands. He envisaged screams, contrasting with the sombrous clowns that sat uttering no words. The devil dressed in a cochineal, Prada jester suit reposed atop nothing, locked to his immaterial chair in a stalwart trance, locked in an infinite stance. He saw two lovers wrapped in their silken amour, and gold duvets, making sweet, sweet love! Above, he saw a starry night stirring, both the argent moon and the orange sun eclipsed, joined to the hip like Siamese twins. God had pardoned all their sins.

Not all of his visions, however, were so elegant. Some were ribald and grotesque, delineating a harlot fellating an unshorn fawn. In an additional instance, Saturn had, recently, been placed in a mental asylum and developed a mania, inducing him to devour his beloved son. It was no fun being overrun by suffusive horrors, and peculiar oddities.

At the start, he was able to cart these negative prohibitions, and shun them to a land bereft. He had, somehow, reached the ground floor. He bore many scars from his tumescent tumbles. He had, nonetheless, attained his fatidic destination - his final destination even.

His hand had evolved; it was as if losing his sight had caused some inhuman mutation within his other senses. He pondered to himself if this was worth all the fleshly expenses? An all inclusive surgical procedure, excepting the physical extortion and pain. When he commenced his endeavours, a spasmodic jerk would occur. He ascribed it to his body acclimatising to its new toy, for he was having too much joy.

The clock struck eight o'clock, when his brush gave way to the friction it had so endured - all day long. Its wheels had burned out. No doubt, so had he. You see, he had been tireless since we last checked his attendance sheet. The canvas was not the sole thing he had been molesting, since, whilst protesting, he had been embalmed by these saturnine feelings.

His laces had been tied to each other with the utmost malice, causing Humpty Dumpty to crack and smack upon the floor. Metaphorically, of course.

You see, Hughes had been enlightened with the divine gift of never-ending inner conceptions, eternising throughout his now fanciful mausoleum, however, these were his illusory deceptions. He knew not what he was, in reality, painting. Was it worth the hassle? Did he care enough to battle for the man in the High Castle's tassel? The pellucid diamonds, gauzy silk, woollen cashmere, and prosaic rhinestones. He had jumped in the wishing well, as a desperate attempt to retrieve his sanity. Gretal had run out of breadcrumbs to help find his way back. He was entombed alive, suffocating in visceral excruciations. He had lost his wits.

He remembered not having transgressed such bounds, but he was the assailant who had cleaved his eyes out of their fatuous little head, as of pygmy gadflies. He had operated upon himself, during a hysteria of bashful somnambulism (even sleep despised Hughes), bidding him to manifest his doctoring of his eyes. Or a shedding of their skin, was the terminology Hughes gave. Toilet paper shawled around his head; he looked like a Grecian deity, without a fruitless velleity. He had given up walking, festering a devolution. He lay sprawled on all fours; he was now one of Doctor Moreau's forgotten projects. He was an ill omen. A Roman mural. He had lost all his neural activity. He cackled; his voice had taken the tone of an execrable witch; bewitched by Shaman Blues. His ego had suffered a mighty big bruise. He had found all the booze in the sobriety of his abstinent home. The highest in the room. Wondrous death and dour gloom. He had finally escaped his mother's libellous womb.

He grabbed the nearest blade; he always kept one at hand, in case of suicidal urgencies. He was not shy. Prepared all the time to take an easy ride, and sail along the Styx to the gates of Hades. Mithering his moanful injustices of triviality to Charon the while they travelled. He took a deep breath, as the train dissevered his jugular veins. They burst from such oppressive strain. Sweet Mary Jane. There was almost a poetic taste to this. For, though his work was always hit or miss, he had now become this bottomless abyss. A fleur-de-lis. The prettiest star glinted her last breath, swallowed her lordly pride, and accepted ineluctable death.

Wishful sin, my children. You can make a deal with the devil, but know he shan't rest until he can revel in your demise. Be careful what you pray for, because it might just come true. Miring you in paralysis upon your loo to spew all your sinful poo. Goodnight, ladies.

Trigger Happy

For our next tale, let us spend the night together. We shall follow the story of a man named Phillip Seymour. A mighty big bloke, and with the tip of his fingers, he could give you a bloody good choke. Nevertheless, he wouldn't hurt a fly; he was a shy recreant. He wore a suit and tie to his occupation. His place of residence was Londinium; that was his dominion. Every morning, he awoke to a slice of rye, and a cup of chai. Despite being your average joe, his taste strayed far from that of a joe. His taste was that of a blonde Wandsworth yummy mummy.

Though his tummy had a large appetite, if I were to depict his general features, I would struggle. He was fair in skin tone, his height was that of a slight giant, ranging at 6.4, his brilliant green eyes gave him a striking glare. His physique was that of a pear. It was such a pity, if he had but an itty-bitty waist, the opposite sex would drool over his forbidden city. He was the last heir of the Seymours, the last of a once formidable race, yet now they had all died out in space. Major Tom called it a modern travesty. He called it modern love.

What has love even become? A broken drum. He often sat glum looking, and leafing through his illimitable dating apps. That was the truth of modern love. His mother had given him a shove to get out of the world, and soar into dating. He had been debating it, however, after her passing, it was his last resort. Talking to a female reminded him of heathen rugby, and a heated scrum. It was no fun.

If I am to be crude, he had never even embraced a woman. Was that rude? Well, fuck it! I couldn't withdraw that information any longer. I felt his sexual repression causing tension within me: your humble narrator. Bottling up inside of me, as if an inflammable pyromaniac. It was like playing hide and seek, but the seeker has died. He had never dared to fondle his pizzle. It lay crestfallen and deflated; it needed not come and say hi. There was no spy who loved him. His enormous trombone stood in stone, awaiting an inch of satisfaction. Alas, it only ever smelt the noisome gas from down under. A Kentucky wonder. It waited to hit the country road, and be taken home.

Can you imagine that, being at the fine, ripe age of twenty-eight, and your ship has never flown? Your ship never left for Coney Island, baby. Your rocket never set course for Funky Town. It lived in a miserable shanty town. I fail to think of the right noun to drown his failure in.

In any event, we have established his sexual disaster. A risqué erotica forsook by rakes, sybarites, and debauchees akin. There is no necessity to add corrosive salt to the already peeling plaster. He was yet to adore doting upon his satellite of love, as premonished in his laughable gospel. Every day, he came home from his crippling job, and spent hours researching, typing, and perhaps, ailing the health of his fingers, insinuating problems in his future. He might require a suture, if he continued. But one day, whilst he was tapping away at his virile keyboard, an advert flashed before his eyes.

Like a shooting star, it glinted ever so bright. I admit, though, it may have been his screen's brightness. The advert was, nonetheless, so strange that it hit his impotent scar so fiercely.

It read, "Are you looking for love? A lonesome girl near you needs a lonesome boy like thee. A lonely girl ready to receive a good thud is looking for a lonely stud like you." He felt a surge of hormones possessing his body. He had never heard such gaudy, haunting yet émotif words. His little Peabody became disembodied with something ulterior. Some foreign diction - it must have been fiction. Ooooooh baby, oooooooh baby. His diaper needed changing. A door had been left wide ajar. He looked from afar, but he swore he would soon enter. He clicked this advert.

He was led to a mysterious website. He had, for the first time, witnessed the sensuality of a female. He had always assumed they had a dog's body. He was stupefied; he had reached the motherland. Wrecked upon some destitute island with but sand to sustain him. At least he would return tanned: a handsome glaze of auburn honey. He began with something insipid, and tame. The caption read as follows: "A Girl meets her maker". How scandalous. They couldn't handle us. Seymour kept repeating himself, reaffirming the meagre confidence he owned. It was a bookshelf of categories, subgenres, literary adaptations, and movie remakes. His hand tremulated, as he scrolled through the lurid immoderations.

He had never been a fan of reading. But this seemed different. It spoke for itself. He impromptu felt ill. Phillip Seymour gave a boisterous cough, and proceeded to unzip his rearmost. He flung them, trying to replicate what he saw in these scholarly epics, alas it was, perhaps, the least titilating thing you'll ever lo and behold. O' Jove. His right hand was placed on his fuel tank. He pressed play. The Freudian male commenced spanking his deviant patient; hearsay told of her having been reprehensibly naughty. Seymour reciprocated their writhing, by yanking the tip of his fuel cap, soddening it till dank. Faster and faster, did Seymour tug, whilst watching this goatish ritual. He chanted prayers of "oooooh baby, oooh baby," evidently aping the words of the female lead in this irreverent, short film.

Why was he empathising with Charley's girl? A cowgirl riding her horse apace. They were riding on Highway 66, following it to the olde town road. I must say, the horse was quite a boatload. Her voice spoke in morse code. Seymour exuded cheerful noises of disembarrassment. What had this petit fox of a whore coaxed out of him? This was a follied pleasure. As his billowing thoughts quitted his ignoble conscience, he groaned and realised he had a delivery from the sordid milkman to cleanse.

He had salivated over a foretaste of a proscribed fruition. Un goûte for tooting his hoot. After work, each solemn eve, he thundered play on another poorly written Broadway. As time enlarged his palette, he came to have masticated over everything under the furtive sun. Each night, he gave a bow and commenced his feast. First, he perused the normal categories of literature, then, he diverted to a lustful of lewd documentaries. Mastering an articulate, conversant, and studious fluency in lechery, as if an imago hatched as a pornographic philosopher. From masochism, proclivities towards BDSM, and euphoric dominatrixes pulverising phalluses - the Solomon of sodomy illuminated like a perverse carnival for carnality. Wherever his freak lured, he abided and adventured hence. His genius knew no bourns, for it projected its ejaculation pearling his feral habitat. Majoring in such a loathly diversity brought much responsibility upon Seymour. After a season, all of the above commingled into an indifferentiable pile. He went to the extent of hiring an aedile to keep track of what he had and hadn't viewed.

From Africa to America, his plane sailed even to the depths of China; he never discriminated. He had rated so many countries now with his ink pen that he no longer knew what to do. He tugged around seven times a night. Enough to give any ordinary man a good fright. Every night his pen was dight to commence the fight. By the time dawn woke, he had no ink left to spare.

The milkman had given all he could share; he often felt a puzzling tear in his ego.

Phillip assumed what he was doing was universal. When every masculine figure returned home, were they not wont to do likewise? If they had a wife, of course the woman would take charge of the wheel, supposed Seymour. Ensconcing their spouses' Volvo into a befitting parking stop. He could not be the sole thot in this vast world.

We now reach the head of Seymour's narrative. The graph but plummets downhill from here, folks. New sensations lead to disturbing temptations within our protagonist.

There is a brand-new dance, though I am uncertain of its name. The people of God shun it again and again. It is large and vascular, full of tension and strain. Lust, turn to the left. Lust, turn to the right. Lust. Promiscuous dooms are seeping in, skulking into innocent minds alike.

In the miserable course of his fate, all Seymour could process was the photosynthesis of his veiny muscle. The tussle with his addiction spiralled. His vertigo became overwhelming. He could not leave the safety of his home, lest he missed out on an anticipated blockbuster. He had transformed into this omniscient cinephile. His comprehension of sexual exploits vanished into a galaxy far, far away. His view on women deteriorated, he saw the false depictions of them on his screen as mere objects, and marionettes, being given their due medicine. Thomas Edison would have hung himself with guilt, if he saw how askew our inventions had turned from their creators. Dragging them into the dark corners of this planet.

The entirety of Phillip's duress had surrendered. His videos were no longer gendered. He had been rendered to resort to whatever neoteric specimen he could unearth. His hand often pulsated from transitory withdrawal, in spite of his veins entreating for respite, alas they did so in complete vain. Speaking of vain, his own self-regard compounded - black tar narcotising his ego awry. His hands had formed impetigo from a lack of hygiene; he utilised both of them, either were apt to wield his twisting sabre. Tectonic friction, too, had incapacitated noxious blisters betwixt his rheumatoid fingers, and upon the palms of his disgracious hands. At least he had become ambidextrous. Quite a talent for our young gallant.

This addiction had perdured for 5 months when, one augural day, a tempest roared. Like any good Brit, he had quit his occupation, opting for redundant hedonism. A man with no aspiration, save for coiling his pleasure dome. It was where he felt most at ease. Today, he must have been on his 40th game of tug of war, prowling through every nook and cranny to find the sublimest fanny. He was steadfast, in deep meditation, when the mutilation occurred. He perched and pondered, questioning the racy film, portraying a tribal orgy of five, fictitious aborigines skylarking a single woman.

Seymour imagined how tight her clit must be. Alas, I must disagree; I don't think he was quite accurate. Regardless he was in a thronging throttle. His bottle was spilling nothing but arid air. There was not a care in the world, besides his beloved degeneracy. Abruptly, his crown was subverted upside down. His string bean went, "Snap, crackle, and POP!" He swooned all over the shop. He even debated giving his pizzle a merciful chop. Sanity, however, absolved that premonition out the rash window; instead, he surmised the superior direction to head in, was galloping to his local infirmity. They were adept in such whimsical, and preposterous, misfires.

When he returned from A and E, his religious credences had been transformed - purified. He swore never to walk on the amatory side of hell again, not even for Sean Penn. A favourite of his. They had forewarned him, by saying: "Look Phillip, if you don't give him a rest, we may need to put him down. It is not always ethical to unman one's pet. On the contrary!" At this remark, Seymour would diminish into torrid chimaeras. He listened but when the doctor, then, hardened his reproof, by exclaiming Seymour's frank gravity: "You're bleeding him dry, we don't understand why! Your French fry needs a good lie-in from time to time. A good bedtime, yes? Or else we might be recourse to emasculating you, Seymour," the word "emasculate" reverberated throughout his mind, usurping his previous omissions. 'Twas then, that heeded their wise precautions and deterrents. He enlightened himself with the resolve of abjuring choice from his sins. His felicity, however, woefully depended upon these cheap thrills. What could be grand enough to cumber him from taking these libidinous pills? Nothing. Lust, to Seymour, was king.

A fortnight passed, where his battlement remained strong. The priapic soldiers, down below, fought the cravings from above. In continuum shoving his wild frenzies, which essayed to dissolve this newfangled doctrine, nevertheless, he was impervious. He venerated his forbearance, likening the temptations to the Garden of Eden. Eve were the films, whereas his desires were the wily serpent. It was important he kept the Trojan Wall guardant. Constant surveillance, in hopes of prevailing equity. His radiation monitor erected every night, uttering soft lullabies. It wrought so hard at spiriting sedition - a rise in our faulty hero. Bleu, blue, electric blue— that was the colour of his room, where he slept in longful gloom.

Waiting for the gift of impending doom. His tomb was already preordained.

It became too much for our hero, he had attempted to go cold turkey, but time flexes like a harlot, and is such a Herculean bore. It created too much chaos, and unrest in our young mistress. He had lost this unremitting charade of chess. He had exerted his best intentions, alas, none can conquer such an unbeatable quest.

Bedlam bestirred for Seymour on a frigid winter's eve, with the frost jeering at his window, taunting: "WONDERFUL, HOW FUN, JUST GIVE IT A TICKLE."

His satellite of love, in a profound dejection, inveigled also: "I won't bite, just come over and smite me. Your curly whirly has not had its medicine for some while. Let's go fly your knight to the highest height; don't be a little shite!"

He put his hands on his ears, resisting and dissuading himself otherwise; his efforts were fruitless. These superfluous trials at denying his own yearns—if he denied it any longer—these would be the ghouls to who forever beset and haunted his disorientated view on life. He arose, and sat down on his congealed couch. He hunched over; his eyes lit up, as if he was Jimmy O'Savilloi visiting a newly opened girls' school; of course, that being nursery for infants; Jimmy never went for anything above prepubescents. They were past their prime, ripened to their expiratory date. Tenderloin steak ought to be rare.

With the delirium roiling around his repulse to succumb, Seymour, hands abreast his cheeks diffusing fretful perspiration, combatted for dear dignity. Alas, he forfeited by yelling: "GIVE IT TO ME BABY, SHAVE ME, LEAVE ME RAW, I WANT MY STRAW BURIED!" With this submission, his wish was granted. For the sequent hours, he rolled, bowled, wrung, gurned, and burned his joystick. It reddened as blisters festered. A pimple was begging to be freed and spew its miasmal contents amidst his room. He had hit the motherload, two-week buildup of pure curdled milk. His shrink would be ashamed. His priest would rebut him of absolution. He fell wanking to the floor; it was almost comical how tragicomical his song was being sung. The bells were rung, and for his time had come.

Formula 1 would have been majorly impressed with such brisk speeds. Vin Diesel would have considered the Phillip family as kin. Seymour had anew begun watching videos he had already seen. He was no fastidious eater; he required but to ejaculate on his pristine wife beater - an irregular sight to behold. Stella, have mercy upon our erring Peter Piper. Stella disregarded such prayers, for his joystick rent entirely off. Gore ensanguined everywhere; it threw itself on his blue walls, apologising as it did so. Sorrow for the morrow, when the cleaners were sent to perform their weekly deterge. It would be a scrupulous one at that! His Jean Geanie had been excoriated for its indefinite final wish. His diving board had been bent to a thrawn slant, from diurnal diving of its Tom Daily.

A philtre of heterosexual and homosexual romance—what a woeful last dance. 'Twas thus, that the integrity of Seymour set sail for France aslope. If memory serves well - Marseilles. He stood up, and observed Charlie Chaplin's cane, realising his circumstances would nevermore be the same after he had just committed. His complexion became one doleful sullen. How ironic that he had been abstemious for nigh an eternity, however, when his avarice gluttoned, like achromatic flowers blooming rainbows, the compulsive hex cursed him with a downtrodden perdurability. His hands were sullied with sanguinary slime, exemplifying the crime, and lacerating it in his face.

Rick James, in a state of shock, put down his crack pipe for he was overawed by Mary's freaky joint. Captain Hook's claw appeared straighter when compared to Phillip's hook. Seymour, like any honourable captain, knew he must sink alongside his redoubtable keel. Regrets I've had a few, but then again, too few to deplore. Alas, I have never snapped my twinkling winkle. Seymour's ireful meat was decorticated raw. He cried out for his own statue of liberty. The young Americans were not content with his bigotry towards his disembodied statue.

"Will all the perfumes of Arabia not sweeten my predicament? Miss Fanny Gill, descend from your hill, this is your fault. I have executed no crime. Why do I whine? Will all of Neptune's formidable ocean not wash this blood clean from my memory?"

His malady saw no elixir to vanquish the lustrous misadventures. Nothing remedied, nor allayed the perennial and exquisite smarts of his penile misdeeds. Urinating alone was a moiling horror which Seymour knew would but further excruciate him. After this hapful affliction, Seymour ere long took his own life. Life seemed O' so miserable without a means to lessen his blood pressure. O' boys, boys, 'tis a sweet thing, such a wanton thing to have perished from excessive frolics. Mickey Mouse grew up as a tyrant; Donald Duck blew up in war - ciao; and do not get me started on Pingu, who passed from a luckless flu. Our dear Phillip subscribed to the likes of these unreal jesters, becoming a mere ghost tale.

Some fear the big bad wolf, others fear the reaper, however, I revere the maneater. Manducating and regurgitating her victims back up, like a teratoid siren. Everyone covets to rein their vices, lord over their world, and not be told otherwise. Here we saw a puny man's vice orchestrate his own device to decease. The jocular element being the fact that our ungainly Prince unCharming never kissed, osculated, deflowered, copulated, or, most pathetic of all, even hugged a female; they were but his imaginary friends. I suppose happiness depends upon the player, but I myself would not want to be the benefactor of such hopeless, novice choices in life.

Before you give it a whack, heed this tale as an admonition that it could crack. À demain my disciples, say goodnight to your idols, and remember to bridle that feckless snake in your diapers.

A Needle in a Haystack

Francois flicked the whetted needle. It seemed pococurante of him doing so. Francois and Roberto had crescendoed upon a strait in the metamorphosis of life where neither were satisfied. Robert was a virginal chrysalis, now mutating into an egregious butterfly. Francois, on the other hand, had indulged in myriads of abstruse drugs beforehand, and knew it to be a frangible procedure. Francois' arms were emblazoned with train stations, ranging from Glasgow to Penzance. A wide variety of British havens. Roberto, by contrast, had never displayed any interest in narcotics. But, as mentioned, the plight of his straitened life had superseded ecstasy, therefore, in the tainted eyes of his chaste virginity, this was his sole remedy of redressing his anguish. Francois' plight was machinated by none besides himself.

Francois had not even essayed to vacillate, or seed doubt into his friend's lusting for an experimentation with the infective skag. He almost found the woe of it all, to be a hilarious travesty. Another factor into his obstinance of suading Roberto otherwise, was that he shall at last make his own guilt subside. Abating whilst his neighbour's fate befalls analogous hate. Francois came from an affluent family, as they often do. He had first experimented with pre-onset alcoholism at the jejune age of sixteen. Pellucid and sunset ethanol, however, were far from enough. The primary instance of Francois quenching his impassioned thirst for the direful substance when he hit the legal age of seventeen; but a year after cascading through the eminent halls of drunkards. The magus in his soul had bewitched him, with an insatiate love for insobriety.

Francois, after siring his idle hebetude, and abandoning his future, was evicted from his familial home, though they offered him a ransom of bounteous money. A pot of gold, as he called it. Alcoholism they could deal with, alas skag, no, that was an impeachable sin. Deep down, he knew their exile was attributable to their own connatural vanity. Alcoholism could be cloaked up with a farcical shade, heroin however, leaves stains on your shirt, veins, corpse, and face.

Francois was preparing their injections, and charring the cinderous liquid aflame. The foul bubbles effervesced through quickening heat. Roberto's eyes gleaming with a coruscant complacency at such a sordid sight. He felt like a guileless newborn, learning facile words. These being, "I devote my allegiance to junkiehood". He took pride in the fact that he was degrading his, hitherto, tintless purity. It negated the turmoil of his crumbling career, and issued a different path to undergo in his tribulations. He knew he would be infatuated with a single hit. That was how the narcotic enthralled a credulous person. Roberto had taken a very prestigious path, studying at Cambridge, and was in the midst of mastering finances, and the chicanery to do business. He had moiled at a bank for a few years, although after losing his mother, he began losing the concept of "how to function" without her. "How to exist in a world so devoid of amity." He witnessed the lung cancer spoliate her prowess, in spite of her never having been a serf to cigarettes. Hazarding with the decline of his mother, he, too, forsook his scholarly endeavours, and after a rapid while was dismissed.

The needle was set, and Francois, under wonted circumstances, would have taken that primal hit. It would be unthinkable for anyone else to contravene his arrogant priority, however, he coveted another archangel. Another companion to sail along the wild inconsistencies of intemperance.

He swabbed the belt tightly around Roberto's skin. It blistered with a sulphurous carbuncle, as veins wept tears of agony. Entreating for more healthful air. His veins commenced to implode. O' how he possessed envious veins, thought Francois. They prostrated in the nude, unaware of the nocuous kisses they were about to be serrated by. Roberto wrenched death by the handle, and axed into the plumpest stream he could see. The narcotic welled sable, coursed his taut vessels, and traversed across his chaste innocence to then assimilate, and spoilate his white pigment to dark-amethyst. Blood oozed out, Blood oozed out, fleeing from the ghastly maws of this atypical septicemia. Roberto's face dulled, puckered, and contracted all in simultaneity. His lips rigidified, as his face glowered effete and red.

His virginity had been effaced off, and in its stead, baptised into a league of knavery. Roberto ruined upon the floor with a loud thud. Silence entailed. Francois was overwrought with joy; he had sourced that partner he had so sought after. Someone to share the rest of their dolorous existence. You see, once bitten by the snake, there was no reversing its tether. You are groomed onto a Cimmerian highway eventuating to nowhere. All you can do as a precaution is fetter your seatbelt, and ready yourself for a rocky road that is not particularly sweet.

Face to Face

I wanted an interview with the devil himself. An up-close and personal confrontation, with the man who scolded the world with woeful fear. Today was to mark the breaking zenith of my career. I was to adhere to one of America's most notorious rapists, homicides, and molesters. Anything under the infamous sun - you name it, he had trespassed upon. A bucket list so long, it would shame the iniquity of any murderous miscreant. In spite of its considerable length, the entirety of this terrific list had been ticked off. He was the paragon boy scout. My circumspections of what tact I would ingratiate, ascended me through a nightmarish reverie, bereaving me from reality. I didn't know what time it was, but my lights were low. A room lit by dim umbras, exemplified my fragile state of consciousness. I leaned and abutted my radio, as Bowie muttered some euphonious lullabies into both my ears, propelling me further into a moonage daydream. This execrable starman was to be the prosperous bane of my career, like a malign, meteoric benison searing through my current failures. I suspected he would be charming, as wont with most awful criminals. About as charming as a freshly rolled joint of Mary Jane - this was no time to humorise my loathings. He had demanded I bring him a packet of Marlboro light blues, and a four-pack of beer. He was imprecise on which brand; therefore, I chose a four-pack of Stellas - shadowing my insolent jest. I pray that they will awaken some inner recluse within him, as if a hermit crab arousing from his inactive carapace.

I drove into the abyss of the tenebrious night. It was a subzero night, entailing that I strapped up. Extra thick, there was no chance of Winter's love impregnating me. As I drove, I imbibed slow but meticulous, sips from my silvery flask. I had never relished the bitter and nauseous taste of liquor. Neither had I ever required a stimulus for confidence, or subside my social anxiety, though when one is combating against a talent such as "America's Most Notorious", there is a prerequisite for aqueous fortitude.

Something to hush the affray of my inward negativity, soliloquising the horror looming ahead of me. I envisioned him, in punctilious diligence, awaiting my advent with a repugnant sneer across his disfeatures. There was an evocative miasma awash the air: bodeful fate.

All I saw were strobic images, flashing in cyclical intermittence, of the crimes he had perpetrated. The road was steep from here, and I heard my automobile, Lucille, stall a handful of times. Even she was struggling to reckon with what we were about to come face-to-face with. As I tried siphoning out my dubieties, a voice kept bellowing, "Turn…turn…the fuck around!" I, of course, neglected these treacherous portents.

My career has been at a checkmate for three years, or so, now. I had injured my slender ego through warrens of pathetic, infructuous interviews. Around a year ago, in a state of professional depravity, when I accepted an interview to "uncover the truth behind Burger King's foot lettuce crisis," the vituperous critics cleft me to worthless shreds.

Shreds of lettuce. Enough with the dour wisecrack from me, I am but essaying to evade my trepidation. That noun flounders to showcase my unease in all its golden glory. A path of glory was what I sought. Coming to your screens next summer, the piteous tale of a desirous fellow desperate for laudable ratings. I had devolved as a New York telephone conversation, gnawing at people's minds. Gossiping all the time. The bells were chiming with Furphies. Rumours, hearsay, and alleged slander of my declining health. I was to shelf these offensive drivels with this grand finale.

They shall all hail me as the new heir apparent to Hunter S. Thompson, excepting the incapacitating narcoleptic habit. I was never one for the intoxication of drugs. My own father was, heavily, influenced by the whole charade of oozing booze from his pores, begetting my chary perspective towards stupefying oneself, and the virtue of temperance as a whole. I suppose the "Midnight Molester" and I had one thing in common. He had proclaimed with vehemence in court about his own parental issue: from his mother's delirious ailments, and of his father's inhibiting addiction to ethanol. I was certain to quiz him upon his filial tragedies. Nature or Nurture was a thesis of mine, which I coveted to be corroborated from these interrogations.

I had arrived at my destination, where my fear now exacerbated into contrapuntal excitement. I was in a gladsome peculiarity; I was never good at conversing with angst lurking behind the feverous curtains. "A phantom of the byline". That's where I draw my line. I took a step outside, and the boreal air frosted my rosy cheeks. It was Mother Nature's way of giving you that maternal kiss; a Freudian paradise - one for luck. I, before ingressing into my mantic viscera, looked up at the gloaming, bespeckled by infrequent worms aglow emitting ferocious resplendences. Extramundane cicadas chirruped their mellifluous dirges. The waxen moon cast a shade of opalescence over Earth; it was beautiful. The cogs of this world seemed amiss, and supplanted for an extraneous, woolly meridian.

I suspired my last morsel of undefiled oxygen. Then, I forged on.

I reached the guard, to whom ushered me forth, towards the reprobates designated room. His sombre smile spoke a thousand silent words. We slithered along the concrete floor. The fretful guard anchored his brawny feet, scraping them against the strident boardwalk below, whereas I skulked like a ponderable panther, being fastidious by effecting my arrival as noiseless as possible. An insectile predator can discern the minutest of sounds. One presageful sentence kept repeating itself, as of a parrot, whilst I approached the atrocious monster: "Merde! Merde! MERDE!"

The door unlatched, and there lay the usual suspect. His eyebrows enlivened with glee, his condescending simper shaped with arrogant delight, and his eyes shined with rejoice. This was his requiem for fame. It had been ten years since the last article about his disastrous rampage was last mentioned. Both he and I knew who was going to be marching this interview into victory. He was the composer, and I was his servient orchestra. It was like a black belt being put up against a white belt. Napoleon, foolishly, walked into Russia with downright vanity beating through his cardiovascular system.

He rose up, and his shackles hissed like a rattlesnake ready to bite at any at any extemporary instant. He extended a fawning formality; I complied with artful reciprocation. His palms were glacial, hallucinatory almost; it shuddered me to the marrow. The kind of shudder when one tramples upon your grave. We were now to commence the hunger games.

Midnight Molester: "Did you bring what I requested of you? If you neglected my requests, young man, we can call this interview off right this second. I was never fond of one party profiting more than the other."

His voice was almost angelic. It spoke kindly, yet with mordacity, bearing a fatherly semblance.

I, in a state of disquiet, threw the packet of Marlboro light blues on the table. It was a footling endeavour to mask my submission already to his character. I drank a deep sip of Neptune's holy juice to clear my dreich throat, before my reply was put out into our feral vastitude.

Winston Camus: "I brought what you asked me to, don't worry. Can I ask, what shall I call you? Saying Midnight Molester is but a slight bit long-winded for my preference."

Midnight Molester: "Call me Charles, my boy, Charles Knox, that is the name on my birth certificate." He manipulated his lineaments to deform a grimace, or a mutinous smile; however, it seemed sincere enough.

Winston Camus: "Sounds good to me, you can call—"
Charles Knox: "Winston Camus, I know who you are, son. Do you think I would let any old sod interview me? I have read the array of excreta you have written. I adore the maladroit fashion in which you butcher journalism. Perhaps I am being harsh, your writing was adequate - five years ago."

I had been put against the cunning grandmaster of chess; he knew my every ungainly move, my every possible move, and each waking thought inside out. For a moment, I was tempted to forfeit, and dowse my frustrations by going to a tavern nearby; surfeiting my sorrows to hence afar off. Why did that thought come into my brain? I had but gotten intoxicated a sundry of times in my miserable life. I, nonetheless, kept my resignation, and pressed onwards with the interview. A career was on the minatory noose, suspended in my fore, swaying…drunkenly swinging.

Winston Camus: "Yes, being frank, my career is plummeting - as you so eloquently implied. You are my last hope. So, let's make this beneficial - for the both of us." I gesticulated a sly innuendo, thereupon Charles nodded in accord; he already knew this was my ultimate hope of redeeming a tainted repute. I placed the packs of four Stellas on the table, kindling his claws to, in immediate succession, excavate them and scoop them towards him. Embowelling one of the beers apart, he then downed. I could physically see the liquid voyage through his gullet, whilst he grotesquely roiled it aswirl, like how a pretentious wine taster in a vineyard would. It was now time for his secondary vice. He grasped a cigarette betwixt his two front teeth, and conflagrated her lithesome corpse up; she set ablaze. Sphering a pygmy fire whenever he breathed in an inhalation. A fawny witch smouldering at the Salem trials of 1693.

I placed my audio recorder down, and pressed play; we had begun. Before I could initiate the questioning, however, Charles took charge of the wheel, as I had intuited he would.

Charles Knox: "I was always rather disturbed, you see. As I am sure you know, my father was an inebriate: whiskey was his lionised form of poison. My mother was feeble, and tottering; many times, she could have axed their marriage, but no. Alas, I confided in literature for a comfitting shoulder to repose upon. I would, of course, ascribable to our financial straits, thieve from our local library. They never caught me, which I am sure led me to believe crime was accepted as moral, or that I was, perhaps, too vulpine for those cunts." He delayed his next scorn, by speaking with tendrils of soot coiling out of his mouth, "Do you wish to add anything, Mr. Camus?" With sardonicism discomposing me.

I could murder him right there and then, when those words left the walls in his mouth. How dare he denigrate! He knew this audio would need to be published somehow, and a comment of that sort is fatal for any journalist's reputation. "Would I like to add anything?" I repassed through the phrase on unnumbered instances, fuelling my fit of rage which was spuming inside my phlegm. I wanted to pounce upon him, and straddle him whilst suffocating him. I would yell, "Who's in charge now huh?!" No, no, no, why did I have these untoward desires? Evil waning my docility. I swore never to be violent after my ex-wife and I divorced. After much quietude on my part, I retained the kettle from exploding.

Winston Camus: "Why thank you for being kind enough to include me, Charles? Yes, I read you liked Dante's Inferno from a young age; I even brought the book along with me for you to, well, read over, for good times sake." miming his identical jeers.

We both were playing a game of toxic masculinity. He was a Millwall fan, and I was a man of colour. Two starstruck despisers caught in a stalemate. Who had the bigger erection? I placed the novel upon the table; it was his favourite edition:

an ocean of vermeil deluging around a diablo - I had unburied some anticipatory research on Charles myself. His eyes beamed rays of genuine joy. His ears, nose, and smile became erect. His cheeks finally gave way to a hue of healthful colour; he was no longer the wretched Snow White.

Charles Knox: "Wh-h-y-y thank you, Mr Camus. Do…you mind if I have a r-eee-aa-dd through?" My God! He was stuttering. He had been rendered impotent; I had won the cock off. He had degenerated to Bill Denbrough, a puny little child, in despair attempting not to urinate, and defecate, their own hubristic diaper. To herald my victory aloud, I chuckled with disdainful contempt. A sempiternal, strenuous, and grandiose chuckle.

Winston Camus: "Why, don't be silly now; of course you can, Charles. Why do you demonise me? I would not be so cruel as to do such an unchristian thing as taunt you with your beloved novel. After all, you are the murderer, and I am merely the journalist."

He smirked at this reply, and like a child bearing witness to their venereal toy, he began leafing through. He even went as far as to kiss the novel. Strange man, thought I. He caressed his wife delicately; this was, perhaps, the affablest one would ever see Mr Knox misbehave. He had reached a page he adored, I could tell, for his brackish eyes were gorgonized to it.

Charles Knox: "This is a glorified citation of mine, my boy, it reads as follows: 'Death is a torturous and inescapable eternal life.' You see, my killings were a rudimentary public service. Only in death can we experience eternal life. In life itself, we experience eternal death. Death begot anguish to hagride the things that it execrated - us, his forsaken beasts -

and life forged the Earth as a sanctuary for such torture - life is mentally ill."

He mystified his dark cynicism behind a veil of verbosity. All the same, he hypnotised my attention, which now axised around his gravitational intellect. I decided to challenge him.

Winston Camus: "Is this your form of justification? You were a Hell-raised cherub sent to deliver the senseless from their state of compliance."

Charles Knox: "You are better educated than I thought, son, but well, yes, I suppose. Once I had read Dante's Inferno, I developed an obsession with the morbid, with death and penance as a concept. I formed this philosophy upon seeing my own mother's state of complacency to her hideous life; I deduced most people were doing the same. I have had many years to reflect on my crimes." He assembled the vestiges of atonement, procuring a horrid disfigurement strewn across his pride.

Winston Camus: "So you have remorse for the countless you brutally slew?"

Charles Knox: "No, don't be a fool. Each one of them can thank me for freeing them from temporal purgatory."

Though he had labelled me as a fool, I could tell from his comment about my education, that his guard had been laxed; allayed under our newfound commonality. He now viewed this interview as, possibly, having some intellectual value for him. I was no longer the farmer bleeding his udders dry. One aspect I admired about Knox, was that he may have been a crazed slayer, thief, bandit, and molester, however, he was the brightest star you would ever encounter. I had become a zealot, adhering to and admiring each syllable that came out his abhorrent windpipe. The ungodly messiah speaketh.

He put his claws, once more, on the second Stella and cracked her agape. Anew inhaling with instantaneous urgency, I suppose that was his way of savouring them. Father like son. He eschewed Dante's Bible aside, and resumed conversing about his crimes.

Charles Knox: "As all killers do, I began with trivial animals, and despicable insects, then the birds and the bees ensued. They were my unwitting test subjects in my operating rooms. I would often try to replicate, or roleplay with them. I would helplessly try to save their lives, but as I am no doctor, they would inevitably perish." He guffawed at these atrocities as of sacred recollections; it perturbed me how callous, and intriguing, he was.

Winston Camus: "Did your mother never suspect, or smell anything exceptionable?"

Charles Knox: "Oh, she did, upon myriads of incidents; she had the features of one who is harrowed by a dawning reality. She would, nonetheless, turn a blind eye; it was my father who cared. He would finish his glass of whiskey, then hurl the bottle at my disgracious face. He was a dreadful aim, though."

I recognised a sense of pity, a sense of melancholic desperation to bless the man with an endearing hug, as a form of condolence. Alas, no, this was a man who had committed too many wrongs. But why did I feel a connection? A sympathetic voice in my head, demanding I give him remorse. I conjectured it to have been a similar scenario in my household, by contrast, with my father being an exquisite marksman. A mediaeval archer with a glass bottle. Blemishing me through a violet moon, which bedewed me with a tenuous silhouette of abuse.

He had perceived my internal emotions, and me relating to his childhood sorrows. The predator had smelt his prey's foible. I could ascertain he would now think we were compatible. He was a lustful man scrolling through asinine dating applications, and seeing me, he swiped right. We were a match. I was his genre of woman.

Once more, he manned control of the interview. He had transformed into a quizzical journalist.

Charles Knox: "Enough about me for a while; I feel rather vain. So, tell me, son, a little about yourself. What is your most eulogised novel?"

I bowed down to his question. I knew, ethically, I ought not to be discoursing over literature with this man, but if it manifested the expedient information - so be it! I would deign to speak on pretensions, and pretences, with this dubious inquisitor.

Winston Camus: "Well, if I were to answer that in earnest, it would be A Brave New World, which I am certain you know O' so well."

He cackled at my quibbing remark. An imbecile one at that, I admit. Of course, the oracle was fluent in such a paramount book.

Charles Knox: "Of course I have read it, my boy, Aldous Huxley, 1932. A very pleasant read. I do like its overarching dystopian message, yes. I think his greatest novel is Island, written scarce before his passing in 1963. It counters the dystopian societal ethics formed in A Brave New World, and creates a more utopian society. It is mispriced and often slaughtered by critics. However, what do those critics know, anyhow? Am I right?" Sardonic again in his delivery. He knew this would besmirch my puerile ego. Instate a laceration on my wounded shoulder. The vipers (a superior name for them) had been the reason for the disputes between my wife and I. She had commenced to traduce me as a failure, a laughable pile of hay. "America's most notoriously inept writer". I remember the night she called me so. I made sure to put her in her due place after such calumny.

I had disfavoured, also, Charles' means of clarifying his erudition of Huxley, by defogging the year of its release, and other boastful insignificances; they were a superfluous redundancy.

I plighted my facial muscles to contract an etiolated smile, so as to react to his jocund snide.

Charles Knox: "If I am to be truthful, I much prefer George Orwell's take on a repressive government in 1984. What an impactful allegory that one contained! He was always a skilful writer. Animal Farm is another one of his indisputable magna opera. The aptitude to mantle one's political, subjective views, within such an enticing tale. Now that's a sign of a superb writer."

I acknowledged his successive poke at my pride, though I was the bigger man. He was merely a school bully essaying to provoke a reaction, and then plead to the teacher of his innocence when things got scalding. I knew this human quintessence all too well. I never had an abundance of friends at school—acquaintances sure, friends not so much. I enkindled a misanthropic, and cynical stance on matters respecting inhumanity.

I felt like moving the colloquy on to a more political controversy to see where we would chance upon. This was one long highway, Route 66, from Chicago all the way to

Santa Monica. From flagitious murder to dissecting the odious cranium of a deranged monkey.

Winston Camus: "Do you care for politics much? I notice that we have mentioned two dogmatic authors, with vivid opinions on the pontifical politicians of our world."

Charles Knox: "Politics, politicians, and the law, my friend, are things I am unaffected by. Whether it be the right or the left, they all derive from the cognate continent. The continent of corruption."

His cadence, as he vocalised this, was mellow. Monosyllabic would be uncouth, however, his emphasis was depleted; it was a stern but amicable reply.

Winston Camus: "I guess we have something in common."

Charles Knox: "I think you'll find we have quite a few comment denominators, Mr Camus."

Queer for him to solemnise me by using my surname name. As much as I abhorred to confess, it was correct, we were affiliated by a few similitudes. I felt an urge to outright repudiate this statement, alas, in truth, we did. From parental issues to literary interests, we had now ticked another analogy off. Was this a job application? It certainly seemed so.

I resolved it was apposite to drop Oppenheimer's bomb on the table. Commence the grim, grievous, and ghastly petrifications, which would hook my fellow readers and listeners. Ensnare the disgustful bait, for it to be reeled back in militance. I had brought photographs of his previous occupations with me, from the circumcision of a man to the vivisection of a pregnant lady and her foetus. In the least sadistic way possible, I wanted it to evoke the most outrageous reply from him. I craved that barbarous, ruthless response from my malevolent gallant.

I began perusing through my leather satchel; my fingers quaked with a concoction of fear, and ardent stimulation. I, with sloth, moved the weathered photographs towards him (I had revisited Charles' uglifications of virtue, on restive eves, and eager morns). He deciphered, in precise, what deck of cards I was handing him. He was to receive a perfuse house of rich hideosity. There were four photographs: his primary murder, his strangest murder, his most bestial murder, and his salient grand finale, before the jury condemned his conviction. Four of a kind. None of these victims were above the age of twenty-one, well, save one.

Winston Camus: "Tell me a little about these, Charles." gesticulating toward the molestations, with a wailful hesitance.

I resigned my tongue from balderdash, I wished for an unprovoked incitation from him. An undoctored anecdote. He licked his lips with one elephantine, circular, rotating loll, and eructated out a roguish bolk; all the more aromatising the milieu to sordidity. It appeared that was his method of expressing arousal. He clasped the first murder by the tip of its neck. With his left hand, he reached for the packet of Marlboro light blues, and fired another sorceress alight. Heedlessly blowing the darksome smoke in my direction. Another form of chivalry from my knight in impertinent armour.

Charles Knox: "When I turned seventeen, I felt I was no longer a wee little teen. My doctorate in beastly dissection no longer quenched my thirst. So, akimbo, I patronised onto more adept matters. I was at a boisterous bar, when I met him.

An argent luminosity swam throughout the confines disorientating one's abstinence. You see, I thought it practicable that I was homosexual. I knew of a quaint bar, specialising in gaiety, but a couple of miles outside the metropolis. Of course, a gay bar would never be permitted to be in the citadel's epicentre, and America would never condone such a travesty. Anyhow, we conversed, he was well, he had some shrewd wits to him, we imbibed, et cetera. I invited him back to my abode, to which we strode toward. Rollicking hands amidst each other's fraught bosoms. I recall the sinuous rays of wan light coursed upon us, as he travelled to his improvised doom. I never set out to murder him. He was more of a…"

Before he finished his sentence, he stubbed his torch out upon the photograph, cindering and discountenancing the departed seraph, depicted in its eternal museum. Etch contrition was present.

Charles Knox: "a propitious stone, shall we say? I needed to experiment. I was Victor Frankenstein, and he was to be my abomination of a monster. We entered my home; I had since vacated my parents' restrictive domicile, and lived in a dwarfish flat, about five blocks away from them; though I had a grudge against my valetudinary mother, I knew she required aid. My homosexual victim's and I's tongues flowed inside each other's mouth, entempesting billows of lovesome lechery, and both our pencils were sharpened for hedonism. Alas, I had a repulsory lapse. I threw him against the bed; to his dismay, it was not an act of perfervid salacity, but more so of wrath. Then I reached for my drawer, where I always kept a meat cleaver, and hacked at his phallic manhood. He bled to death, like a rainbow swine."

As the words marched out of his stairway, which was his repugnant mouth, he prized his right finger on his left nostrils and heaved an enormous mound of idiosyncratic mucus onto the floor. It was vulgar. The bilious venom was of claret colour. It seemed his years of chimneying had caught up to the old bastard. I assume he had contracted some sort of respiratory canker. I now fathomed another layer to his reasoning for this interview.

I suppose this was an addition to our growing commonalities. We were imploring for a requiem to excel us to immortal redemption. The pied piper would fiddle his flute amongst his amassment of prenatal children, incanting both our bequests.

Winston Camus: "W-w-w-hhy did you not end his suffering there and then?" I was thwarted upon a sensation joying me astride his awful reveal.

Charles Knox: "In all honesty, it was cowardice. I feared the repercussions of terminating someone's existence at first. Seeing his blood seep down, like an animal gibbeted in an abattoir, was 'righteous'. In my eyes, at least." the avidity in Charles daunted me; perhaps, I was enabling him again to resurrect his malefactions.

I was imbued with virulent detestation. I needed the toilet to purge me of this undomesticated nausea. I needed to flush these sinful sentences out of my head; most of all, I yearned for a drink to even me. If my mother had heard this, she would have wrenched him by the ear, and "washed his mouth out with a bar of salubrious soap." He seemed somewhat remorseful, but only for the fact that he had not ceased the homosexual's escapades there and then, not at the butchering itself. I went ivory as snow; a hemicrania loomed, as though it was slipping into reality's doorway. Not now, this necessitated a hundred percent of my prowess. Acidity began to surmount up my oesophagus; a hot, liquid, and molten mass rising upward. My fire brigade tried, in haphazard desperation, to proscribe disaster; nonetheless, it was too late. I vomited my dragonite exhalation upon the floor.

Charles Knox: "Sensitive stomach? I can be less poetic, if you would like?" He chortled as he said so.

Winston Camus: "No, no, do not spare any of the details, please, I insist." I held back another wave of acid reflux. In this instance, I triumphed.

His ogre hands, once more, hoisted the next pornographic adversity, however, before he started speaking of the next diagram, he dominated the third can of Stella.

Charles Knox: "Mr Camus, son, do you have a key, a house key? I feel like giving this a good shove down the old gullet." he gaped toward me, with an expectant inflexibility.

I, with reluctance, slipped him my house key. He sundered the can open - from the bottom of its arse - and sapped it of its blood. Dracula sucked the poison dry. In a matter of three seconds, the ethanol had been ingested. He was once again ready to renew his grizzly tales for gruesome kids. He tightened his unruly grip.

Charles Knox: "Continuing on, this elfin sexual exploration - my fiendish erotica - led me to the conclusion that, no, I resided not as queer. Thus, after a few mercy killings, I deviated to women. I found solace in this. I had unsheathed my requisite orientation in the 'lgbtqrstklub' as a heterosexual."

That comment brought a smile to my transparent, apparitional face. I had to give it to Charles; he vivified me with easeful hysteria; neither I, nor the audio recorder desired to confess so, but it was the emulous truth.

Charles Knox: "I began with a similar technique—bars, booze, and uproarious intercourse—before slaughtering them in my perverse workshop. I remember there was one winsome woman, hmmmm... Ellen Ripley, I recall, was the name on her driver's licence; I relished her so much that I allowed her to live."

Winston Camus: "Why do you think this is so?" His apish hands scratched the flea-ridden disguise of his face. He was in deep perplexion. Brooding on his past negligence—the one that got away.

Charles Knox: "I suppose I saw too much, dare I say it, content within her own life; every night, I frequented these bars, I confabulated with incalculable men and women. I did not sanction a randomiser on my appetisers. I, meticulously, chose them. I looked for the snickers amongst the Mars bars. The pellucid diamonds amongst the nebulous rhinestones. She appeared to be a diamond, however, when we returned to my abode, I noticed that she was far too rapturous and conversable about her 'future aspirations'. I think she said she aspired to become a lawyer - why mar such visionary hopes."

My research had uncovered a file on this very woman, who, after the murders had taken place, decried saying she had almost slept with a serial miscreant. Yet he had wrought some fallacious excuse, forcing her to be evicted from the flat instanter, before their lust went any further. And well, she had indeed become a lawyer, a reputable, prominent, and prestigious lawyer. I retained releasing these details, to obviate the possibility that he may regret the choice he substantiated.

Charles Knox: "It was one evening, at this bar named 'Tropicana', that a woman bearing a child was slumped on the barstool, being harried by lecher after lecher. I could distinguish tears swelling in her crystalline pupils. Crystal blue. As blue as a vintage New Orleans record. The gaudy illumination of the establishment etherealised her the more; as glinting serpentes coddled her cerulean orbs. I was in thrall, and not for the sole sake of plundering her apart. I could, nevertheless, scent fatalism within her. I approached her, with sincere curiosity. We nestled abreast, and talked for hours, until the barman told us it was time to quit from the premises. We returned to mine. She wept until dawn radiated. I felt so much compassion for her. Her husband had been philandering with wenches for months; prior to this adultery, he had impregnated her with ecstatic, wistful dreams, and a child. Upon her questioning his loyalty, he fled to a faraway realm, evanescing from her presence. I declared it a clement time to engender this woman's legacy, ergo, I operated on her and her infant. I effaced her puny mortality, and surpassed her to continental stardom. She was as illustrious as Marlyn once was. I fashioned her so." Circumscribing his grievance at ignorance of humanity for misapprehending his deeds, Charles cavorted his distaste in blatance.

He now articulated his annoyances, and even sentences, with indecorous rage. I had not negotiated his ideals of 'creating a legacy' for her, nor had I interjected him during his recounting of his factual story; notwithstanding, he worsened as supercilious with this narrative. In his twisted mind, he "owned" her. He was Metro Goldywn-Mayer, and she was Judy Garland, pumping her with toporose narcotics to sustain her serfdom. My mind was unhinged; a screw had flown aflutter. One sip of courageous liquor wouldn't hurt, would it? Oh, I oughtn't, I never quaffed on the job, not since, no. But one singular sip to but quench my longful palate.

Charles Knox: "My boy, I know these woeful anecdotes inflame angst within you. How about we share a drink for these next two?"

His vainglorious attitude had hazarded an excellent presumption. How had he deduced my tragedian turmoil? He unriddled me too well. What had given me away? I opine, with his father and himself being rather gluttonous alcoholics, he knew the expression of a man who hankers for intoxication. I did not kneel to his suasory will.

Winston Camus: "I am afraid I don't have any, Charles. I never drink on the job." He smirked, he saw through my fiction.

Charles Knox: "I have smelt the acerbic gin from your pores, ever since you sauntered in here, Camus. I never was one for gin; I was a whiskey man personally, as was my father before me. No sane man interviews an insane fool, sans a drop of liquid valour. One won't immobilise, nor stupefy - will it?"

He voiced his temptations through heinous yet wondrous prepossession. Tenderising his words, kneading them as of bread, eventuating a direful instability in me. I combatted these wicked defects of mine, and reckoned with the consequences of relinquishing them. I envisaged the translucid aqua fructifying my throat, and saccharifying my confidence. I could withstand his cows, and perturb him instead of the current inverse. Perhaps it would benefit me?

Winston Camus: "I-I…suppose not, Charles, I suppose not."

His entrenching of my obstinance had succeeded. I followed the sergeant's orders, like the sanctimony of the gospel. He was Dieu, demanding me, his fair Abraham, to cohere to his outlandish solicitations, an inimical bawd straying me otherwise. I was to murder my morals at the head of an irreligious altar. One excitation from my glacial flask could not warrant any malice. After the real ephialtes I was being forced to digest, it would avail me to again screw that bolt firm in its stead. My mind was a blackboard, and spirits were but a delightsome eraser.

I turned the metal flask's cap round and round, till it impugned its vehement seal. It entreated me to cease, though I always disregarded imperatives such as "no", or "stop". I could have sworn it was stuck in a clockwork motion for what seemed like an eternity. Whilst I was preparing my defiance, I perceived that all his attention was now upon me. He wanted me to adulterate from grace, and be a godless reprobate. He smote me with his iron mace, and I scuffled to wade past the injury.

I took the first drink, which felt dissimilar to when I was fortifying myself, whilst in the automobile on my erratic journey here. In these circumstances, it felt couth, and proper, devoid of that former self-abashment. I was succouring the community with some justice from my service to the bottle. All exult the mighty bane. A fruition superseded my previous acrimony for Charles, I dampened my pessimism upon his iniquity. He had enlightened me with a venomous renaissance. I began to perform miniscule but vigorous wolves from my flask, for the remainder of our rendezvous together. He, too, conjoined me in my insober affairs by riving open his final Stella.

Charles Knox: "Cheers, son!"

His voice thirsted for me to view him as familial; view him as an estranged father, met by professional chance. I sensed that we were solemnising, and distancing from commonplace punctilios. This filial veneer did not last more than a fleeting transience, as I bestirred myself back into reality.

Charles Knox: "Let us have a brief interval from all the ribald gore I am plunging us into. What do you think, son?" He punctuated son by dispelling a steamlet of thin smog, volatilizing into our disconsolate ambience.

I nodded with acquiescence. I needed a break - needed a kit kat, as the untuneful advertisement says. My mother had always adored them, whereas me not so much; although always recollected their hackneyed slogan. Some slogans but stick to your fibrous cell membrane, mauling at your cognitive reveries. Before Charles thieved me of my thunder once more, I drove my masterdom into the parking space where this barbarous octogenarian, who could scant walk an inch, sans her ivory cane, wished to.

Winston Camus: "What music do you like, Charles? Heavy metal? Reggae? You strike me as a classical man."

Charles Knox: "Me, classical, no, son, I like, well, my father and I loved Little Richard. He would gyrate his records on his stridulous cassette. It was about the sole instance of us "bonding" - so to speak. My genre was that genre of music, and the Blues aplenty. I grew up down south, after all, where the insidious sunset blisters unsuspecting people."

He had annexed that inapplicable, and predatory comment, for no plausible cause.

Charles Knox: "How about yourself? Let us speak more about our interests; it allows me to see the broader mural of who you are."

I discounted this curious comment about "the broader mural", and attributed it to his florid figure of mysterious speech. He had a pompous eloquence with words: an elaborative and symbolist diction, unwonted to the ordinary man. Then again, he was no ordinary man.

By uttering his juvenescent remembrances, Charles had forged a forgotten key, and unfastened a pathway within me also. Little Richard had been a welding point in my father and I's relationship. I could recall one summer's eve, a scorching and sultry one at that; tensions were insufferable, and as was my fierce father; "High on life" he would call it, when fuddling a handsome liquorful of crapulence. I had been bereft to my own devices, and my curiosity took over.

Whilst he amounted to surplus arrears at the doctor for skeletal problems outside, I was enslaved in anatomising through his Little Richard CDs. I had discovered my disposition, "Send Me Some Lovin", therefore, I proceeded to get my pygmy, corpulent sausages all over his CD. Foolishly, it played at its maximum volume, raging through the soft walls of our home. Good golly, Miss Molly; upon hearing so, the tyrannous ogre roared, and beset homeward into his putrid bayou. I had an impure-amethyst of the eye for a fortnight afterwards, tumefying with each consecutive day.

Winston Camus: "My father and I adored Little Richard, too. 'Send Me Some Lovin'' was always my favourite."

Charles Knox: "'Midnight Special' had a special place in my heart."

Though never my immediate choice, nor my remiss second, nor even forsaken third, I admired his unusual candour. I had often surmised my father's proclivity for Richard, as one of their homogeneities: both engulfed in parading their dipsomania. They say polarities attract; however, my experience has been that similarities stick together. Stick like the atrocity McDonald's hoodwinks as "veritable cheese" upon their dank burgers; or, if malfortuity arises, then it can be wizened, as of a longevous eld.

It was time to crusade again along the pilgrimage of death.

Winston Camus: "Shall we resume your relaying of events?"

He had been waiting for me to hand him the microphone. To hand him an aureate globe, an Oscar for the dexterous Mr Knox. The hunchback of Notre Dame smirked, and pressed onwards. He flicked to the third photograph: the rape and molesting of Penelope Schnider; I suppressed my exigency to nauseate on the floor. He blazed a match from their invidious chamber, and inbreathed the chimney smoke, expiring through onerous and calculated intermittences.

Charles Knox: "Well, I had now crossed sanity with the debasing of an enceinte belle. I needed something vicious, affectless—something to make Sid squeal!" he bellowed, without realising how much his tone had augmented, "I began hanging around infantile playgrounds. Mothers are so careless, so unchary of the feral beasts, which skulk the Earth unawares. I witnessed miscellanies of ripe subjects behoved for the deplorable crime. I meditated on a particular misfortune, one who would leave an imprint after martyred. She possessed flaxen-brown wires, hair wisped like Medusa's disgust, yet she did not palsy you to implacable stone. She did, however, incite your rock to indurate adroit. She stood in the frozen ataraxy of childhood, waiting for me to swoop her off her feet, and espouse her to the house of pain. I could picture Barry White serenading her into awe. She was—"

Winston Camus: "How old was she, Charles?" I swooned against the vile horror of his tale; his elation, discernable upon his visage, infuriated and repulsed me in concurrence.

Charles Knox: "No more than three years and two months."

My face contorted, he had handed me a feculent and mephitic warhead - a sour lemon, and an acidulous glass of limoncello. The way he so depicted this child with insouciance, for her to be but less than conscious, she had not even the mental capacity to decide what words to use in conversation. Her brain was on autopilot, as if insomnolent, and memories were hebetated in hoary ice.

Winston Camus: "YOU SICK-FUCKING CHILD MOLESTING PER…"

Charles Knox: "Mr Camus, your language, please! We have an audience, do we not?" deriding me with the facade of gentility. His contemptible aura of nicety was issued to me, through a guileful hypocrisy of sardonicism, and an ugly lour.

He was right, however; I must spite my tongue, no matter how execrable his transgressions were, and are still. I needed to prove to people I was not a violent delinquent, as the vituperous press had calumniated me to be, after my wife and I parted ways.

Charles Knox: "You know the saying, don't you, son? If their age is not yet on the clock…well, they must be begging for that manful cock."

My veins disfeatured my face, albeit I resigned my enmity from duty, manacling it down in anticipation of receiving electrotherapy, if it dared susurrate an additional objection. Impartial was the laudable mode of conduct for such trepidant ordeals. I looked straight out of a Dolmios advertisement—a swollen-cochineal complexion.

Charles Knox: "I shall pretermit the gratuitous details for once, as I see this is a sensitive subject for you, Mr Camus."

I disdained when he employed my surname, I thought it implied his assertion of hauteur upon me.

Charles Knox: "I letched for something that would affright that plumb reaction of which you just produced. I was tired of the same repetitive Hollywood Studio films, machinated with the lone intent of profiteering; it was time for a masterpiece, to dwindle all the servile pirouette to my genius. Thus, I gave the world Penelope's mangled cat. You see, Mr Camus, as Kubrick once said, 'a painter paints, a composer composes, so a director must direct', ergo, my comrade, a murderer must murder. I was an artist in my days. Are you much into art, Camusy?"

No one in my forty years had called me "Camusy". He trampled upon my dignity, and unyoked me immobile to his thaumaturgic torments. With his libel of my character, I almost omitted the absolute face he had pronounced to me. Justifying his malefactions as glorious feats of excelling contemporary ingenuity. I opted to resist the provocation, since everything he said was a cunning ploy to gall me.

Winston Camus: "I am fond of art, yes, I used to love Edvard Munch's inanimate faces. My wife and I went to Oslo to see his series: 'The Frieze of Life'. I was mesmerised by 'Separation', the way the sepulchral man grasps at his atrophied heart, knowing nothing will, or could, ever redress it again; juxtaposed with the woman in white, whom is given no facial individuality, she is purblind to their nuptial schism."

A candle inside me had become incandescent. A delicate hue of fawny magnetism. I had, with no vindicable purpose, spoken of art - from Little Richard to Edvard Munch; I felt as though I were speaking to my old lecturer. We were intimate, he took a parental role in my life. Guiding me to follow my creative passions, which I never followed through with. Don't most dreams end up blearing into an irrevocable nightmare? Was life not but one labyrinthine swimming pool, with us, in vain, attempting to stay afloat; therefore, we empower ambitions to dull out the inward disgrace. The internal failure we live amidst. Dejection within societal constructs is always upbraiding its slaves.

Not only had I blathered on about a masterpiece, but I knew I had just given away a vital piece of information to the devil: the dissolution of my former marriage. He would manipulate this to his warped whims - I was adamantine of so.

Charles Knox: "Your wife, Camusy, how is she doing? Must be lonesome tonight without her prince charming."

Winston Camus: "She is used to it by now. She knows I am a hard moiler."

Charles Knox: "Why do you dupe me all the time? Camusy, my son, I, as I said, did my own research on you before you came. I did not need to do much undigging with your wife. The fathomless crypt she inearthed you in after the divorce was profound.

One of the foremost headlines that appeared on man's technological invention - the satanic internet - was of your scurrilous tendencies."

Winston Camus: "I NEVER LAID A FINGER ON HER CHINNY CHIN CHIN!!! FALSE RUMOURS, FALSE TESTIMONIES, ALL FALSE, FALSE LIES!!!"

I had disempowered my personal shield; the chivalry had descended upon my nescience. He knew of my crimes, my accusations, and my domestic offences. Damn the internet! Then a tempest swept by, and eased me with usurious respite: Perhaps we were not so disparate. Perhaps I was his mere disciple. Had I assaulted my wife? I know you are all wondering if the hearsay is veristic. I shall deny you the satisfaction of knowing, however, what I shall denounce is that crone got what she sowed. She was no more than a risible, unchaste whoremonger. A phantasmical sentiment was foreboding me with a speculation: Charles had effectuated our tryst, as means of expediting my sanity to be demented. I felt as though he were incubating me in an impressionable embryo, indoctrinating me to hatch afresh as a devious foetus. Inherit his legacy, and be the brilliant prodigy. I ought, no, I must remain unimpeachable.

Charles Knox: "Relax Camusy, I judge you not for your previous sins. We have all done wrong. Lucifer, be witness to our crimes. He is forgiving of his children."

He reposed a hand upon mine, whilst he smouldered a cigarette afire; a warmth irradiated awash my consternation, somewhat abating it. An urgency to complete our interview dawned across my cognition, however, Charles being surreptitious, sheared us away from our fundamentals.

Charles Knox: "Have you never sought compensation - imagined the avengement of your ex-wife's injustices?"

I stammered at his audacious remark, eliciting that I succumb to gladiatorial criminality. I replied with a toadying nonchalance, as if revenge meant nothing to me, when, in reality, it was treaclier than primordial dew.

Winston Camus: "No…those seditious and amoral thoughts do not inhabit me, Charles." Aspersing him seemed doubtless the apt behaviour. His hand did not veer, nor desist, from mine.

Charles Knox: "Let me rephrase, then. Do you believe in each earthling belonging to a lot of divinatory weirds? I am harkening to its archaic definition, not alluding to its necromantic supernaturalism, or extraterrestrial meaning."

I ogled at him, with an insipid drollery.

Charles Knox: "Are you a man of unorthodox superstitions? I ask thus, since I am. Very much so."

I waived my resilience against his unlawful scourges which flagellated my hardihood. I had already buttressed myriads of his delusory mazes, could it be so difficult as to buttress a scarcity more?

My riposte was to challenge him.

Winson Camus: "You are manipulating me, and being downright flagrant about it, too. Subtlety might aid your cause."

Charles Knox: "Why be subtle? I am illuminating you of the umbriferous cozenage you abide by. The ventriloquist, investing you with your fate, shall determine your serendipity. I am the mere suspect, trying to undeceive you of your repressive fantasy. Man's supernal idiotism is how he can beguile himself of this potential. Convalesce your repression, son, and be transported to your destiny."

I subjugated my helm by carousing in a revelation of ethanol from my flask, baptising me with furious zest. I thereby domiciled in mumchance, and suffused myself with sequent sips, until Charles knew he had forayed a layer of my feverous enzymes off.

Charles Knox: "You envy me, don't you?" He persisted to boast and flaunt his "intelligent" craftsmanship when tackling with persons.

Winson Camus: "I maintain no such jealousy." Taciturnity exudated out of me.

He blew a fuliginous maelstrom of soot into my proximity, and reclined farther back. Laughing with mischief awry.

Charles Knox: "Envy is not jealousy, though let us omit your clever diversion; everyone envies, whether it is inconsequential, or inordinate. The hateful sentiment is engrained and connate, like an incestious inbred bequeathed from forefathers and foremothers akin."

He glared at me, glooming me with obscurant foreshadows.

Charles Knox: "Have you ever experienced the sweet fulfilment of sanguine. No. Nor beheld the vermillion pallor of strangling a person amort - your barbaric hands girdles and controls their breaths. Visualise those hands entwined around your wretched old flame - extinguishing her! The mirthful dominion gained by such pleasure, gratifying you as their veins encrimson. Enacting your abhorrent superiority whilst in coitus. The iron taste of blood pouring out its ventricles. You have felt none of these marvels, and yet, I can hazard at your famine for them. Fear has a face of grotesque allurement."

As much as I despised admitting, his averments reconciled me: the vivid delineation ravished me with serene dread. An infatuation for his premonishes were enthralling me to yield. His conceit aforethought to seduce me into the current amour of unhinging my conformity, fertilised a beau ideal within me. At last, someone understood, gladded, and pardoned me. My whole existence, I had been a wanderer on the Isle of the Dead. Death had immortalised his melody, upon his ceremonious fiddle, for my wake. I puckered my face, masking my endearment for my soul mate. Pope Innocent X had taken me under his judicious wing.

Winston Camus: "Shall we resume?" maundering along an unbalanced beam, "Tell me about your final crime. Tell us."

I spoke with the utmost sobriety. I wanted to assuage him back home. I was unlike Hansel and Gretal's despiteful parents. I was kind, cordial, affectionate, and spineless. In an instant, my grudge would be spirited with the wind, even if you had sinned. Charles rejoiced at my newfound philosophy towards our masterclass.

Charles Knox: "Well, my final mercy killing was my mother. She was the reason for my initial spiral down the levels of hell. We had organised tea together, and I arrived at twelve pm. On the dot!

"She limped towards the door. Opened it, and smiled at spying her beloved and disturbed son. I pushed her to the corner of the room, and began seizing her, throttling her to and fro. This was requital for the years of inadequacy, incompetence, and mortification; she was to reap what she committed. For twelve hours, I forced her to endure horrid smarts. Every now and then, she would supplicate that I bestow 'Mercy', or in flamboyant bouts, she cried, 'Charles, please, please, I raised you,' she endowed me with neither of the two. She gawked at me, as if I had alchemised into an ecclesiastic, and she, she was a sycophant, praying for me to assoil her trespasses. Of course, I did no such thing. Mercy was not in her vocabulary. Mercy would have been to abet her benumbed child. She was no mother. She was no woman, either."

His vexation started pollinating through the distressful milieu. It nettled and corroded like mustard gas, but was as deadly as Zyklon B. It was prepotent enough to be used in Auschwitz. I suspired deep, protracted, and enjoyable breaths. His personality was now coursing through my lungs, my airways, and my alveoli. I had been corrupted, bastardised to his dissolute leagues, and transcended my pitiable life. I knew my destination. I was no longer a wraith wandering the Overlook Hotel; I was as fabulous as Dan, and as maniacal as Jack.

Winston Camus: "Really moving stuff, Mr Knox. One final question for you, Charles - if you do not mind me calling you so?" He nodded his approval through a jovial gurn, "Do you have any regrets?" I quaffed an outrageous amount of liquor from my flask.

I knew his answer already, since we were both now interfused. An amalgamated faecal virulence of illegality. How could I not know what circulated that debauchery of his? I was toying with him, and in fine, wanted it for the record.

Charles Knox: "Regrets are for the faint-hearted, my boy, I have had a few, but too few to mention. At my decaying age, none shines so brightly as to blind my everyday life. Thus, in effect, no."

I ceased the circumlocution on the audio device, leaned over, and soddened Charles with a humectant kiss upon his left cheek. He bleached, and then reddened with glum humiliation. It must have been the first affection he had received in a while, besides the occasional dropping of the soap in the illicit washrooms.

Winston Camus: "Thank you, sir, thank you very so much. I am grateful, and forever at your behest. I shall make you proud fat—" I regressed from denominating him as an idyllic father. I was yet to attain his prowess, therefore, it seemed akin to insolence.

He was dumbstruck, nonplus drooling from his saliva. He tried to countermand my statement, however, I had already skipped out of the room. I strolled down the corridor. I was no longer a passenger, riding and striding through vacuity. Galloping and galloping around the merry-go-round. No longer stuck with cruel existential aspersities. I was free, like a bird unchained from its tree. I began humming a tune I had shoved away since my French education in primary school: Les Enfants de la Patrie. It reverberated throughout the echoing halls of Fort Knox.

Le régime de Vichy would have lynched, emasculated, disembowelled, decollated, and quartered me. La guillotine would have been blithe, comparative to Vichy's merciless torture. Sous le ciel de Paris, I had become a compeer of the bourgeoisie. I had climaxed to the zenith in the song, where we are told to "sourire un peu", and trust me, I had the most officious smile upon my shorn transfiguration. I gave the prison doors a sweet roundhouse kick, buckling it to my mettlesome thew.

Daylight stirred ajar through luminous diminutives, as the nightman was in the midst of unthroning himself. The pearlescent moon suspended still, saluted me by winking, and genuflecting his zealous veneration for me. An ominous nightingale sang ballads of commendation. Everything dwelling in amity, had been supplanted for maleficence. Evil knighted me as its precious kin. Twinkle, twinkle, my little stars.

You know what the clownish element was? I had come to redeem my career, and in doing so, I had recast my whole life. All I was missing was his flaccid love. All I longed for was the love he gave; all I ever knew was his phallic siring Charles taught. Jesus was a false prophet compared to Charlie Chaplin.

The greatest jugglery the devil ever juggled was wheedling humans of his dormancy, sleeping within each and every one of us.

I enfranchised my engine apace, and played Comfortably Numb by Pink Floyd - the only song I could bear by them. My mind mused and refracted, like the sides of a prism; kaleidoscopically musing. I hastened off into the faint offing, contemplating which bar I was to beleaguer next, and what genre of woman I desired?

I pined for when I was going to extinguish my old flame.

You May Now Kiss the Mistress

I portend you, this tale
May make you frail.
Ergo, heed my omen.
On guard my fellow knights
And let us march into battle.
Infidelity,
It could never be me.
Now I sure ain't no Cupid,
But I sure do pertain stupid.
Alack,
Some men are not happy with their wife's ass.
Their bosom fit for kings,
Yet still, prefer multiple flings.
This tale strives to showcase love:
Modern love;
So, give your sexual desire a shove
And let me quench your perversions.
There are many versions,
But today we conferred on Punch and Judy.
Judy was rather moody,
Yet was the finest of wives

Her love as divine as the Maldives
O' so luscious!
They once were the most elated couple.
It was not very subtle!
Kisses, caresses, and comfortable silences;
These are amongst some of the joys they shared.
They had such an endearing alliance,
Les enfants de la patrie
Leurs jours est arrivé,
Leurs jours d'amour!
My flattery,
Does evade their martial battery
As it always does,
Their Roses wilt to Marigolds.
Love is a symphony,
Both composer and orchestra must strive in unity.
They must be a genial community.
Nevertheless,
Some people care not for longevity;
And soon their relationship turns to an abscess.
Light turns to dark, love's spark
Rides away in Noah's ark,
Never to be rekindled again.
Trouble in paradise city.
Tora! Tora! Tora!
Oh, how he bores her!!
They walked the line
She could have been mine, alas nein!
A woman of immeasurable pleasure
An island full of plenteous treasure!
Was that oaf's princess;

His rightful mistress.
I get the Folsom blues
When I peruse such beauteous muse:
Judy was the daughter of darkness
Such a temptress!
They spent five years tightly woven to one another,
Before Punch had tired of a singular Judy.
He chose to smother another mother
Punch morphed into a groupie.
On the 25th of December
He wrote to Father Noël:
"All I want this year is booties and boobies,
I wish not for any material goodies,
Just grant me my wish for some kisses
From another missus."
The previous Christmas,
Judy had given him her heart
Alas, the sequential day, he gave it away!
He thought this as commodious blithe,
Yet it was rather tart,
To stick his goods in an ulterior lady's shopping cart.
Nay, this was indecent for winsome lady grey.
BAH CUMBUG!
Our gallant even put milk and cookies beneath the tree.
This was his plea.
He clung to desperation like a lewd flea.
Why he did not end their fealty is beyond me.
If I were him, I would have gotten upon one knee
And told her the troth thus for free,
Yet some scowl at the thought of honesty.

On the first day of January, her true love gave to her
Deception.
Krampus,
With his mighty compass
Navigated the seven seas
To see what he could row,
Row gently down his wily stream.
He now was the Lord of the rings
Balancing multiple fannies
Mind you, none of which were grannies.
At least he had demarcated some marges.
Every man has his limits
And Punch never wasted a minute with senescence.
His chamber had now been refashioned
Into a crepuscular dungeon of lust.
Ready for him to continuously thrust,
Thrust his golden dust!
His gingerbread men;
A hundred metre sprinters;
Millions of wife beaters.
His fetishes deteriorated as more and more obtuse:
From whips and chains
To bashing their brains;
Vascular veins would strain under such exquisite pains!
He had become animalistic
Zoomorphic, even prehistoric.
Risqué images no longer cultivated
His appetency aslant.
Behold Jurassic Park's neoteric exhibit.
There was one time
I hearkened this from a friend of mine,

That he utilised a ropy cucumber.
He encumbered it forthright up her juniper.
Rumour has it,
He was a fiend for rearward angle parking.
It sent him astride barking!
He never was one for flirting
Punch much preferred a liaison of tongue to tongue conversation.
Skin to skin contact.
It was all a part of his queer act.
He was a man of sparse words,
but made up for it in other ways.
I might sound abstract,
However, the fact is it would detract from this extract.

Punch had become quite the plumber
Pimlico adored him;
He was a newcomer.
He had arrived after this summer,
Nonetheless, he could bang a good set of Hi Hats.
A natural-born drummer.
His signature was the money-shot
A skilful archer
You knew when he was set for departure
The ladies would be left with a form of adventitious present.
A viscid maquillage whited their skin,
Belabouring an extortion to clean up.
His love gun left a trail of snot
It even outshone Gary's snail trail;
He was a true gent.
He always enjoined their consent,

If they accepted - none ever reproved the offer
- they were showered with a thick storm of hail.
Hoary with a chance of lascivious snow
Hoe, Hoe, HOE!
Whilst these women were receiving their medicine,
Judy was too ignorant to put the pieces together.
Too besotted by connubial benignity.
The jigsaw lay neglected,
Despite his breath having an undying, piscine smell.
Oh Judy, how could you not tell!
Incompetent of perceiving Punch as unfaithful,
She collected these negative premonitions,
And ejected them.
It allowed her to be disaffected,
She was so disconnected.
Poor woman, she was being infected,
Infected with doubt, malice and misery
O' how humans can be spiteful
It truly is frightful!
It is so unrighteous of Punch, the philander!
Judge Judy trailed along with her existence,
Or what prevailed of it.
It was not till an inimical springtide day,
In the midst of May,
During a weekly mother's meeting,
Where she began greeting
The animosity he bestowed upon her.
Karen, a garrulous and odious cynic,
declared she ought to insight a bit of fright
Karen, through her oracular cynicism,
was a wise gorgon

Emblazoned with sallow locks
Goldie chicken pox!
May lord have mercy for her hirsute minge
It made every man daunt as craven.
Some bruited it to be bewhiskered!
Likened to a vaginal mythus.
As Karen endowed strength into Judy,
something visible sparked alight,
The Payback was a-coming!
A brown man named James,
Who overheard their querulous complots,
Suggested to put some spice into his rubber bands;
Changing the tempo of his rhythmic exercise
The dance of the spiced plum fairy
Ooooo scary!
A man's iron rod
Is his everlasting masculinity;
Sans it, he is a fraud
A flawed sod.
The Holy Trinity is comprised of:
His sword and his morn stars.
His wood stands adroit every morning.
The witch's resolve was
to send the welkin above to Mars;
This was to be no sweet treat
He would be eternally mourning,
As if an epicene widower neutered.
A black eight-legged creature
Trepidation was about to tread
Off the wall,
A flaming zippo aloll

Firing up the vicinal tree
And letting his kite fly ashore.
A tyrant of an emperor might cry:
"Off with his phallus - to the bloody chambers, he goeth!
Why should he be allowed to beat his meat,
Whilst all she does is sit and weep at her feet.
Justice cometh,
And like a bedazzling comet,
It will blight his lickerish armour!
Fret not, he shall nevermore harm her.

That eve, Judy stuffed the turkeys with poignant chilli,
And in swift, attired her revenge in her lavishest robes.
She spoke in moribund codes,
Her dialect was seductive,
Deductive of her habitual nonsense;
She was seductively destructive.
Verdant velvet, stockings knee high,
Hair ruffled with malign purpose.
Punch, upon espying this glory,
And beset with a lecherous folly,
Felt like being an erotic machine to
His verdure, emerald, and forestry quean;
All ready and clean.
He got his slingshot out,
And slipped on the flaming ring of fire
Holy smokes and sex's jive!
They began thrusting,
Brutally combusting,
Brutally corrading,
Till a gory dusk scoured no practicable reversal.

Our Squire yelled in fanciful balderdash,
as his gloom engulfed with a mauling gnash,
"Fiery! Salacious! Prickly! Picante!!"
His tyre was flattened.
His pizzle quelled
Intoxicated with agony,
Like a thousand stings from a gnat,
With no apparent gain,
As if racked by a dandyish gauntlet.
Judy had what victims of marital perfidy
- the sad hearts of lonely mademoiselles -
Call a vampish moment of divine requital;
She sufficed being a charity.
She relinquished her shame from a man untame,
And apprised her quittance from hence.
But first, Punch needed a wild beating
Thus, upon the raw meat searing ablaze,
She launched herself atop.
She would not cease to
straddle his piebald phallus.
Screaming,
"I'm going to fuck you raw,
Your straw will be in awe,
All the times we shared,
I would have thought you cared.
Alas, You needed more than one lassie,
To chew your grass.
They said it would pass,
However, instead it grew like a cancerous mass,
I am a nubile woman of class,
And thou deservest not my red cherry pie

So, baby, farewell!"
Your star has twinkled for its final adultery.
I'm going to leave with a scar"
– O' did she mar Punch a scar.
She arose from her wailful horse,
And with Arthur's club,
Swinged him of his pride,
Like a God from Norse
Her club struck his band of gold.
Bang! Bang!
She mashed his potato till
Even Freddy found it crude.
Punch would always win the fight,
Though now, his baby shot him down.
Bonnie had liquidated Clyde
His manly soul had been sold,
The fecund DJ had been wrung,
And his last toll had been rung.
The hangman gloated,
The doctor claimed the Dodo was dead.
The reeve turned the other venial cheek.
And Lucifer let out a stupendous roar,
ruining to then masturbate upon the floor.
So, all the prudes
All the young dudes
Take with you these clues:
Once you choose your muse
Be certain to love her delightfully
For she is your quean.
Take her northwards
And treat her like a pretty teen.

But don't be mean
By thirsting for that rakish sheen.
Insert your Richard in but your gingerbread dauphin.
Make fidelity great anew,
And pirthee, stop being a masculine roué.

The Three Stages of Grief

Act 1

Eric had looked despair straight in the face. Clawing at the serrated poignards of a tiger to stay afloat, alas, nothing seemed to assuage his misgivings. He had resolved on a pivoting choice, whispering that it was now time to experiment with something besides negating his tribulations. Depravity is such a travesty, but the real melancholy was neglect. He was prepared to unbosom his manure onto an indubious soul. He had heard of a quaint man, who charged no more than fifty pounds per calmative session. The world of therapy is an expensive pastime, which to pursue, requires a superfluity to expend.

Both Eric and his spectral alienist conversed over the telephone, and the man on the inscrutable end seemed eager to sire Eric under his wing. Eric, nevertheless, attributed his avidity to benevolent sincerity. Certain souls are haunted by the fear of being perceived as rude. Eric was, at the best of times, outright crude. They were to be acquainted for their primal session in two morrows. During these two interims, Eric played pessimistic riffs on his guitar whilst pondering where his issue derived from. Where did the root of his sad tree of grievances originate from? I suppose that is why we subject ourselves to therapy.

Today entailed their day of allying. Eric's wagon wheel was about to roll in miserable merriment. Smoke, smoke, chimneying down the lane. He awoke that morning with a pounding megrim. What an irritant shame!

To soothe the megrim, Eric bewintered his visage with frore icicles, which, contrapuntal to their gelid temperature, thawed him astir. Bursting the soporous blood vessels, which were cowering away from the duties ahead of them. Startling his exanimate corpse with the momentum of a supernova. In unremitting fervency, Eric lacerated his fangs as he stared at himself in the inclement mirror. He was no Tom Brady, but he was sure marketing himself as the finest NFL player to ever wander across America's piteous recreation of an English sport. The inward serpents traduced him, defaming his confidence askew. They wished to avert him from his voyage to the midst of dormant griefs. In ordinary circumstances, Eric would have forfeited to his mental opprobrium, however, he wielded the luminous star of fortitude. The path to acquittal laid afore his keening solace.

Once Eric had concluded the morning customs in his lavatory, he glared into that pellucid mirror, and he, in earnest, spoke, "Take it as it comes, one step at a time, do not let the pressure drop."

His poesy would have abashed the immemorial Coleridge, the Marquis Byron, and perchance, Percy's hymeneal Frankenstein might ire aflame at such pathetic rhetoric, nonetheless, the thought was there. That is what counts. He coiled his nape with a silken tie, crafted from the deities unbeknownst: it was begemmed with motley embroidery, polychromatic patterns unseen by human eyes, and divine to sensualists and puritans alike. He solemnised himself with the finest garments he could locate. This was his ascendancy to glisten with brilliant diligence. Needless to say, with the circuitous pomposity of enrobing his hesitancy with jewels, a suit was his next venture; he was treating the session as a betrothal. The bride soon to be wed: sanity. You may now kiss clarity.

With a sombrous expression, he descended his flight of stairs; his burst of joy had expelled elsewhere. The iron weight incapacitated him, some mendicant pauperised him to privation to the bowels of Hades. A natural-born Hellraiser. Our fair Changeling entered his oxidised Vauxhall Corsa. Manic depression may not have been the lone thing our knight needed to be evaluated for. The keys thrust forth into its mechanical womb, issuing a boisterous cry, whereafter he twisted them - to no avail. This futility proceeded awhile, until on his seventh attempt, the indolent engine jumped into first gear. He drove off into the tenebrious fog, with drab tendrils of smog enveloping any person who dared oppose them; Eric braved such frivolity. "Paradise by the Dashboard Light" began to resound from the Corsa's antediluvian speakers. Paradise was the aim. Gaiety was the game.

He got out of his automobile, with premonitions awash. A palmful of inhibitions and maligns beckoned him to turn around, and choose the recourse of homeward evacuation, though he knew this was what the recreant leans towards, and scampers in cowardice. To be a righteous man, Eric ought to weather inner consternation. It mimicked a passage from the Bible; bearing semblance to "Ephesians 1:7-8a": "in him we have redemption through his blood, the forgiveness of sins, in accordance with the riches of God's grace that he lavished upon us." This influential therapist had converted Eric to neglect two of the ten commandments already. This incognito must be a tempter in a sanative disguise, for in Eric's reborn philosophy, he saw this nebulous man as his saviour, his indomitable redeemer, and his false idol.

Eric arrived at the door. A stern, bleak, yet alluring forestry-coloured door was erect, guarding this therapist's privacy. He knocked thrice, with piercing stridency. The door, instanter, flung agape, and the therapist stood there - an angelic figure, with a hazy gloriole wreathed in his rear. Light encircled him, and a sphinx lay before Eric. It was clear this man was soigné, judicious in his appearance, and tasteful respecting his impeccable demeanour; his clothes being of not a gaudy and superficial kind, but remarkable in their rudimentary splendour. Politesse, as the Parisians uphold, was exuding from his shorn pores. The curative man extended his hand out for a firm masculinity-to-masculinity handshake. It was the building block of any male's prepotency. A lionhearted handshake was a tell of one's character. Too loose and flexible, and the recipient was deterred with an improvised odium, however, too stalwart and tyrannical, and the same procured. A common punctilio, maintained throughout the realm of rakish gentlemen, is that too loose general is regarded in a more acceptable hue. It is not supercilious, like a suffocating wrench is.

The grip of an outlandish Essex lad, and his three sizes too small, unbefitting turtleneck, personates a python using its meticulous theorem against you. A clever species, they are.

Therapist: "Well, you must be Eric. Lovely to meet you. I am sorry I did not disclose my name in our emails, and the phone call. It is a matter of principals, and confidentiality. I am Friedrich, do come in."

As their hands were entwined, a solicitude Eric had not felt since the passing of his elderly woman arose from the grave. His hands were bathed in the most superb of moisturisers, as supple as a babies' hindmost. The grip of a mother nurturing her kindred neonate, letting the infant feed from her weary breasts. A Freudian relishment begot from within. Eric sensed himself to be submerging into a sham idyl of his own abode.

Eric: "Thank you, sir," fawning with adulation.

Therapist: "Sir? For God's sake, why the formality? Just call me Friedrich, or Fred. I may be your therapist, but I sure as hell am not going to discipline you," as Friedrich pronounced so, he scrutinised the garish extravagance whereof Eric comported. He was curious of the kingly raiments which Eric comported, though he knew he could not inquire.

They both chuckled with beams upon their faces, as their infantile bond fastened through laughter. Not forced, not for idle show, simply a severance of repressed emotions. A consensual exchange between two adult men. It is puzzling as to why the word "sir" had been used in conjunction with thanking Friedrich. Though this was placed under a sleek Oriental carpet, he did not want this to taint their sparse time together. Nor for his insecurities to gnaw at him; a verminous rat manducating and wearing at his, thus far, the mettlesome resilience.

Eric progressed into the cathartic chamber, where they were to discuss the philosophy behind his melancholia. He was astounded, since he had never beheld such a mesmeric room: there hung paintings he had not seen since the ripe age of eighteen, when his torch for artistry fired at the merest mention of masterdom. It is but around adolescence that one's visionary imagination can appraise the sublimity in sages erstwhile in existence. As we wane into latter life, the faculties wherein we whilom possessed wilt by no fault of our own. The biological sphacelus encumbers the lively cranium, and necroses the ardent and boundless feats of olde glory. By espying these relics of youthhood anew, which he had admired so, a taunt of the foregone was animated. He ossified time itself, and opted to peruse through insentient hypnosis. He forgot that Friedrich was even present. His glance stole across each mural: There was "The Siren" by John Waterhouse, "Judith and Holofernes" by Franz von Stuck, and above all, the supreme "Garden of Earthly Desires" by Hieronymus Bosch, with whimsical nymphs, rascally faeries, and mischievous imps frolicking in a halcyon landscape. Bosch's artwork had been so prestigious in his manhood, and juvenile years. He always kept a dishevelled replica in his decrepit wallet. Awakened to their congenial reality, Eric retrieved his imitative embarrassment out of its hibernation, and showed it to his novel friend. His mouth swung as of a painting in the wind, transfixed in awe at such panegyric harmony.

Eric: "I-I-I have admired this painting for the entirety of my upbringing, loo-o-k, see." quivering as if blustered by a glacial whirlwind.

Friedrich let out a rather adulterous smile. Eric's puny comparison of a shrivelled mimic almost bemocked his superlative version of the piece. Never smite another man's precious pride with levity.

Friedrich: "Ahhh, yes, yes, what a coincidence. It is fantastical and beautiful. To conceive of such ethereality, requires genius of the utmost," disfavouring a continuation, lest he be further besmirching, Friedrich spoke, "Anyhow, sit down. I have brewed a pot of tea for us to indulge, whilst we get down to the less indulgent matters. Now, before we start, let me bare the essential rules of how my therapy functions. This session, to be frank, is all on you. I must be elucidated with what is amiss. After, we will have two more liaisons, and on the third, I will query you on whether you would desire to consecrate another three. I prefer to operate in triads - I was never one for monogamy! I am no roué, though, I promise."

Eric feigned hilarity, when, in truth, he was dumbfounded by how his counsellor jested on matters of importance, with such flippancy.

Friedrich: "You will see me take continuous notes, do not worry, I need to, so as to get a sort of tenor of how I am to serve you, so to speak. So, when you're ready, just give me a rough sketch of what plumb harries you in the insidious gloam of your mausoleum." A An eerie and tenuous dagger scythed through Eric's confusion. Ruminating at length, arching his spine in a queer posture; he had become Rodin's muse. The Thinker had augured this would be deposited on him, and had thought of some ideas prior to now, notwithstanding, diagnosing the exact blight was a goliath task. Tears were eschewed away, the manful dame toiled with strength, yet with each fleeing transience, the introspections enfeebled the more. Alas, he knew what was to be said, he knew it would come across in a lachrymose roil of pity, almost incomprehensible to a normal soul. Nevertheless, therapists were abnormal souls, they were afflicted fauns.

Eric clutched the handle of the teapot, and poured himself a cup of the black, insipid tea. His eyes locked on the Niagara Falls, which seethed into his magnificent China mug. The mug had Asian swirls, a lilac dragon environing, its luscious pliability acting as an insubstantial fluidity. Once the cup had been filled, and heeding decorum, Eric placed the teapot down, certifying that no seepages occurred, and reached for the full-fat lard of milk.

There was, also, semi-skimmed, but he cared not for its hydrous consistency, as if a maudlin tragedy, which evokes nothing save animus. Eric, from his first rendezvous with such herbs, was particular about how he inebriated the floral beverage: he measured in precise how much milk quitted its keel to swamp his spouse. No more, no less, than the designated mandate. Only the necessary amount. He, then, clutched his metallic, spherical wand and stirred it aswoon. The cauldron commingled from the sablest of nights, embrowning to a chocolate umber so sweet it could transport one straight to the diabetic sanctuary. He raised his chalice, making sure no malice sullied the regal carpet, gave it a titanic puff, and sipped at his nightshade. He was now ready to commence the rapturous suspense.

Friedrich, in the meantime, had occupied himself with subtle condescension. Friedrich resurrected a quiescent pendulum by thwacking it; peeling and lurching, the device equivocating in cognate fashion Eric's frets.

Eric: "I-I suppose it began when my father left us," a rheumy tearlet was insufflated back down, "You see, I was always a fragile boy, but that was where the foundations had been laid. If he had stayed, we would most likely not be here. And you see-"

Friedrich: "How old were you, Eric?" dinting his dole with a ruthless nescience.

This was an artful ploy from the circumspection of our astute therapist. By utilising our protagonist's name, Friedrich rendered him extramundane. By willing his baptism to his volition, Friedrich owned Eric; he was his servile property. Another material accoutrement to brandish in his office. Another painting suspended on the gorgeous and tactful wall.

Unaffected by this arbitrary advancement, Eric continued with his prologue.

Eric: "I must have been no older than 6, turning 7. But yes, I mean, it did not truly settle in until much later; the mind does not really latch onto such things, or fathom them when so young."

Friedrich lolled his contemptuous eyes. This man thought himself quite the psychologist, and scholar, when he was but a quixotic farceur masqueraded in a studious illusion. What did Eric know of the mind, for Christ's sake? Pardon the heathen blasphemy - I try ever so hard.

Eric: "As I grew up, the dubitations swelled and castigated; the flood gates were unleashed. Then there was school. Oh my, the bullies, the bullies! Children are so cruel. I can remember when I was pissing —- excuse my language, but…"

Friedrich: "For profaning, you're going to have to put a penny in the jar," employing a sardonic gravity.

Eric, perplexed by this extemporary regimen, gawked in vacuity. He was to be charged fifty pounds, and now an additional charge transpired for profaners. Was he at Sunday service once more? He never much enjoyed church, for its vastitude of pious catacomb bored him.

Friedrich noticed this baboon's incompetence to decipher a simple witticism, so he decided to abate the perceptible angst.

Friedrich: "That was a joke, a blague, as the French dub it. I see, like the French, you have a wondrous inaptitude for humour. I couldn't care less if you cursed like a madman, I am here to listen," he flailed his pique, demanding that Eric rejoin.

Their quondam religious bond had been subverted apart, and their differences rent as blatant. Eric did not even bother forcing a facade of laughter, he recognised the moment had deceased.

Eric: "Oh, right, yes, where was I… Oh yes, well, to cut a long story short, the bullies seized me and lanced me to the ground, coaxing me to sodden my scholastic uniform, then, to salten my virulent wound the more, they grabbed my head and shoved it in a toilet. Upon my head being cocooned in the sordid and chalky canal, the mutinous leader flushed its mechanisms and the swirling feculence frothed around me," sniggering as if a puerile concubine, "I laugh now, but it was not so comical to an eleven-year-old boy. I can still recall their names: Arnold Vilestein, David Copperfield, and Jim Stark. This was one of the myriads of torment I suffered at school. I have no fond recollections of my education."

Eric paused, a spark of brooding substantiated; he peered into his recessive past, and he saw a metaphorical glittering prize across the Berlin Wall. As he did so, he strained his spinous chord by reclining towards his physical prize aglitter. He heaved another colossus sup, quenching his thirst momentarily. The bitter amber coated the walls of his mouth, and the disconsolation of this inordinately bitter tea remitting his mind the conscientious acridity skulking.

Eric: "I remained quite recluse, avoiding asinine parties, and boozing—all of that teenage dream-like crapulence. I eventually exited from my self-imposed alienation, when I flourished at the age of seventeen. I am not sure why - I just did. Still, the fatherly strifes lurked in the shadows, but I was able to distance myself more from it. Then, when I was at university, I became besotted with the culture of party-sex-drugs. What a lifestyle, huh! A connatural hypocrite, the credence I had so rebutted, was to be pledged thenceforth in sacrilegious glory. This rock-and-roll theology I subscribed to, fouled my salubrious outlook, and shrewd method for studying and focusing on work. I loafed around, and laxed my erudite rigidity. I remember there was a time when…"

Friedrich: "Eric, I do not mean to be rude, however, we must press on to the significant grit in this session, we have but twenty more minutes. Enlighten me with the stressors that, which I presume, came along."

Friedrich said this with a tone devoid of malignancy, he was averring in disingenuity. Time is such a valuable item, one we can never reprise it back, once it has been estranged from your lovesome arms, it has left forever. Time is but a charlatan. It pleads of its loyalty, albeit when the malaise induces grievous ills, it will spall into a million fragments, leaving its partner with distrust. Eric: "Sor-r-ry you are right. Well, I started struggling to balance myself on the vertiginous edge of reality. I no longer knew where I was headed, or that my mental state was about to be impounded amongst mullock. My friends were all fake. Hollow simulations of humans. We had no similarities or commonalities, no comradely topics of interest to converse over, thus I had no one to confide in Besides my rocket fuel of vices. I was a rocketman riding a rainbow of exotic nasal inhalants. Alcohol, to a degree, dissolved amidst the other intoxicants; it was not the worst of my addictions. Nor the most detrimental, health-wise.

"The direst of straits became my marital bewitchment to cocaine. I would wake up, and white my nose with the maquillage of a lonesome clown, stupefying me back into an irrevocable abyss. Before a lecture, an ivory slug would be respired through my nasal canal, uplifting my senses and enhancing my ability to rapidly type the information being hurled at me, by a zombified lecturer. This bled into much of my adulthood. Desolating my once enchanting marriage."

Friedrich: "Let's talk about this marriage, Eric. When, where, how, what, and whom? You fill in the blanks for me now, be a good boy and don't vacillate with me."

The jejune colouring book was denuded. Eric's occupation was to heave wild feu d'artifice, and create something daemonic on the page. To form his own Mona Lisa, his own Garden of Eden, and be ensepulchred in his own charnel as a requiem of traducer asperse him. The coffin had been set, and he now plunged himself wholly into the ground, and sailed east into the oblique Haar. Eric's face crimsoned, it had been a few years since he had discussed his sole marriage, and sole erotical deviance. It was almost as if he was revisiting this chapter in his book of debauchery. He had mystified his theatrics with he and his divorcee, rolling afresh in each other's fleshly excretions, something he had much yearned for.

Eric: "We met at university - both yet to be unbroken into the epicurean panorama. At our introduction, we synchronised our pullulation together, we were platonic friends rollicking around in our own 'filth'. Upon graduating, I took it upon myself to consummate our benefaction to the next peak—a legitimate relationship. Of course, me being me, at the time, the night before I proposed that we romanticise our bond, I had fuddled three grams of Colombian washing powder into my system, experienced an insomniac nightmare, and scarce could I open my eyes. All the same, I queried whether she would flirt with my affinity; she, of course, said yes. The ironic factor was how much I perspired, whilst doing so. I looked as though I were a paedophile. At least, to her I mustn't have. She ensued by entreating that we celebrate, by deadening our comestible appetites. But I had to decline, since my physical state that day was excruciating me. Besides, in honesty, I was far from hankering to eat. The perspiration proliferated, and soaked my entire outfit, hair, and even my penis. I tainted our relationship from day one. We were together for ten unbearably long years, most of which were extremely pleasant.

"Nevertheless, I could never shake my addiction. I'll skip forward, as I can see you want me to."

Friedrich's glare incurvated, his avaricious pupils dilated, and his mouth gaped, absorbing oxygen to replenish this expletive tedium. He exhaled it, with the uttermost discretion, back towards his opponent: a congruous method of bestowing flagellation. Eric countered the jab before it whipped—a sage move from our grandmaster.

Eric: "We married and had two daughters. They were my stronghold, my Fort Knox. Alas, they were murdered by their mother. She proceeded to hang herself afterwards," Eric's tongue was recumbent with a baleful despisement.

Death, if attuned with one's acute ears, was whistling his mawkish flute; his elegiac repugnance reverberated by virtue of the canorous bells from Scheol. They swayed back and forth, imitating that of a Christmas carol, yet Ebenezer Scrooge insisted on it being disparate to the universally eulogised commercial carol. The psalm we have all heard a thousandfold. This statement was foundational work for a therapist. This was the aureate glint which he had been longing for—the instigator to his woeful paramountcy.

Eric had braved the trepidant affection of mentioning this atrocity aloud. His garrulous words heretofore were palsied by such effectual vehemence; slipping from their deathly haunt with ease—no stuttering, no beating around the blazed bush - he had disambiguated their droning antipathy. Upon Eric's denunciation crossing the Pacific into the sedition of our gallant counsellor, a kindly bond was incubating again. Not because Friedrich could relate, but because of unfeigned sympathy, and hence, he coveted to amend him with commiseration. When a man loses the unmaidenly woman he so very much adores, a piece of his heart is spurned into the wishing well; alongside the illimitable other fallen swains. The magnetism of Eric's calamity, was that horror of his seraphic wife bastardising her maternal solace, and slaying her offspring as if they were expendable. The fatality of his beloved foetuses alone suffices to animalise a man to evil, but concocting both of the above, is an egregious recipe for resurrecting the hebete monster itself us all.

Eric: "It was soon discovered, after those years of partying, that she was eluding her maniacal ailment. The doctor declared her to be schizophrenic, after her untimely suicide. I anon spiralled into a kaleidoscope of incessant gloom and despair, and my ego began to erode. I was a solitary ghoul wandering the str-"

Extempore, the as yet silent pendulum deafened the still air. It was the hour of the clock delineating their discontinuation. It was time for Eric to wade through the labyrinthine disgruntlement, so as to unsheathe the chapter of sorrow.

Friedrich: "I am so sorry. I really did not think we would have to end on such an abrupt note. I would say you could go for ten more minutes, but my next client arrives in five minutes. You bid fair to feel the wounds festering, though do not be disparaged by that. Let it not deter you from being so candid in our next session. Through your candour we can unmanacle you, and permit you to wander in the mead of manumission - free from contrition. You did plumb what you ought to have - laying it plain and unpretended. Perhaps, essay not to dwell on the irrelevancies so much," smiling as he concluded.

The frank frontier of dividing necessities and nugations dismayed Eric. He wondered what merited being labelled as a relevancy? In fine, it did not reconcile Eric with an emotive quietus, rather, it exacerbated his bafflement. His certitude resided in the flesh weeping from his raw wounds. He had spewed his rueful entrails to the man, and this man had swinged his confidence asunder with Charlie Chaplin's bane. It was as if, during this fatiguing hip surgery, the anaesthetic had been miscalculated, and he had awoken mid-schism. Grinding, grinding, grinding till his entirety was mutilated.

Eric, also, felt as if, upon his return to his crestfallen abode, he might terminate himself there and then. He was relapsing into a sporadic deluge of dolour. He drowned the residuum of Neptune's golden tea, and stammered over to the egress. He had banished the cordial art of confabulation. He discerned that inexorable megrim emerging again from his Mariana trench. He clenched his jaw, and articulated his farewell.

Eric: "I suppose… I will see you next week…then."

The door was then slammed in his face, entempesting a dispiteous adieu imprecating his mildewy soul. His only thoughts were of iniquity.

Act 2

Eric was aroused to a nervous frenzy: delirium tremens, bodily and thorny pangs, gnomic vision blurring, and everything you abhor ere proceeding with your dutiful therapy. He was troubled with the cyclical pangs of nettling grief, which, at last, saw the resplendent aurora of a vernal forenoon. He performed his analogous wont beforehand, as he always did, however, in this instance the mirror did not besmear him with false slander. The week had been the most exquisite in unprecedented seasons. The last time he had felt so suicidal was at his mother's funeral, three years ago, a year after the loss of his filial family. O' how his life perjured him astable!

Today, Eric was unconcerned with aggrandising himself in his gaudiest suit, and tie, nor combing his unruly hair back into a Presley-like shape, instead, he went au naturel on this scintillating day. Upon glancing out the window, he beheld God weeping—tears of joy, of course. A pathetic fallacy could not have been so pathetically flagrant to its protagonist. He was deserted in his own farcical world this morning.

Whilst cooking his breakfast, his eyes distended towards the flame that brewed his unctuous eggs.

The steam from his cup of tea perplexed him. His wits were amiss. He was a Neanderthal, a space odyssey questing for an indeterminable famine. He had broken through to the other side, where one wishes not to sojourn too long amidst. If blue was a person, Eric was that shade of melancholy. Voltaire would have declared Eric emotionally impaired. Fear and suffering are a sphere of guttering doom.

His chariot arrived, he lunged himself forth into its easeful vessel conveying his insatiable lust for Friedrich's front door. Dissimilar to their previous inception, Eric thwacked one singular though harsh knock. The clock struck twelve as he did so. The paramedic opened the door, with a mendacious grin of, as a philosopher would term, "arrogance".

Friedrich: "Eric, back already!"

Eric looked bemused, and yet again failed at fathoming the most menial of jests.

Friedrich: "I am just toying with you," purporting a remorseful understanding, when deep down, he deplored his idiocy for humour, "come on in. How has your week been?"

This toy was not well received, the roles had been reversed. Now Eric ran on eggshells, crippling his stability, he could cowp in brevity. "Beware of the vex dog" laminated across his discontent.

Eric: "In all honesty, better than usual, I think this could be working."

This was deceitful, there was no troth in this declaration of cozenages. His corpse was felonious on three counts of unprovoked treachery. His lie was as see-through as a Cyanogaster. A slippery fish with clear duplicitous intentions.

They strolled with wry gaiety, as if airing the pretext of homosexuality, to their seats and sat in congruity amongst the habitual pot of tea. If they were to delve further into Eric's psyche, it would not be speaking to a concrete mass, it would be a two-way relationship.

Friedrich: "Well, Eric, I think I will commence by saying that last time we charted the dark terrors of your past, and opened them for conversation. "Would you agree?"

Eric held his inflammable zippo under wraps, his thrusters remained in check. He knew to "keep calm and carry on", as the trite adage designs. O', what a direful expression. Printed on every mother's painfully self-same Facebook page. Each enshrining that they are superior from their neighbour. Alas, each carbon copies itself - the Matrix modernised into our contemporary epoch. Eric: "I zealously agree. I must ask: so today, where will we take this session? We have laid the foundation, and how will we fashion its first floor?"

Friedrich, having a proclivity for metaphorical nonsense, laughed in accord.

Friedrich: "I have written down what I consider the stressors, and I will bring them forth, and ask you more in depth about them, so we can have you meditate upon them."

Eric: "That sounds argute to me - would you like to man the procedure?" a sardonicism was hidden beneath the intrinsic nicety.

Friedrich could deduce the advent of a novel protagonist. The son of Sam had lorded over, hounded Eric, and yielded him into submission, so as to redress his puny ways. A new, stern, and unmerciful phantom sat in his naturelle leather armchair. Nevertheless, being a therapist, Friedrich had to smother all his enmity, and efface it, as though it were never condemned aloud.

Friedrich: "I suppose the first stressor, and in my eyes a very ominous one, is your father leaving you at such an embryonic age. Can you tell me how you feel, or any sentiments towards this acidulous bereavement?"

He was correct, this was the dreariest of stressors, as black as twilight, and as dark as the galaxy, nulled of all stars that drift amongst the cosmos afar off. This was beyond good and evil. This fugitive comet had caused mass extinction for Eric's premature development.

Eric: "I must admit, it pains me to reflect upon it. I look into that historic mirror of myself, and ogle at a person who has been scolded by his father. A man who seeks to be like him, yet yearns to taint any fond and tender memories he has of him. The portentous clock harkens me to that momentous epoch. The moment that debased my life into a tragedy, and I, the lone thespian in its comedical pathos."

He spoke with much suasive rhetoric, entrancingly pending his watch back and forth, ensnaring his victim inwards with his grief. This was music to an alienist's deviant ears, they needed fuel for their cinderous fire, and this was the fossil fuel required to ensure the boat buoyed afloat. Each syllable axed down another layer of the lamentable ozone. Soon, no SPF would protect any wretch from the barren truth of a depressive reality. Existing is not without its faults, there is always a fault in our coruscant stars.

Eric: "I used to thirst to be like him, however, he perpetuated his maltreatment of my mother; he may as well have tyrannised her through electroshock therapy, for the torture she endured was enough to crumble any inviolable woman. Moreover, he was a serial adulterer - this always corroborated my moral compass, and determined that fidelity, for me, is vitality. I think the irony here is that I literalised that a bit too far. I never affianced again, nor even copulated up with female after her suicide."

Friedrich: "This is perfect, Eric - I can see lovelorn heartache spewing here. This is, indeed, what therapy is about."

Eric was bewildered with the honesty he had evaporated into the mouth of mania, although the affirmation from Friedrich fulfilled any resistant qualms. He had been granted the brittlest bone a dog could slaver off. He reposed for an impermanence, pausing to decide it was behoveful for a cup of bitter tea. He stooped into a trance during the process of moiling it. He took a sip, and all his problems melted away. An intangible respite permeated across his lethargy. Eric's conscious vision strayed from gazing at Friedrich, and purloined some of their precious whiles, by embalming himself in the epic painting: "The Garden of Heavenly Desires". He dissected its grandeur through individualising each character: absorbing the poesy of his grassy verdure, backdropped by the whimsical nymphs, rascally faeries, and mischievous imps; however, on this occasion, their visages brightened all the more. The congeniality of their blithe fornication, and malingering of life's monotonous errands. He hallucinated that he saw his shadowy, superimposed upon the painting: he was skylarking with these mythical creatures, through the monsterful leas of Bosch's nonpareil. There is, alas, but a sad finitude to swimming in the beauteous dwams of one's profoundest chimaeras. Eric, transported back into the abhorrent present, and both impassioned and emboldened by the fanciful enlivenment of his favourite artwork, forsook any hesitations of delivering the candour to Friedrich, and nothing besides candour.

He, once more, embarked on the recounting of his misfortunes.

Eric: "Growing up, the loss of a fatherly patriarch made me appear rather queer. I clung to my mother, and assimilated her feminine attributes which, in turn, effeminised me. From the archetypal vocal cords of a dandyish craven, to certain didactic choices, even to how I strutted about the place. My gait was preposterous! This must have made me a bullseye for little kiddie winks."

It was unsettling that Eric had opted for such terminology. It affrighted his remedial partner into being unnerved; it was not the ordinary person's choice of depiction for a youthful child. All the same, he had to abide by the hair of the rapacious dog molesting him for aye.

Eric: "My father left me with scars, he left me with a raging addiction. Whether this be sugar, nicotine, alcohol, drugs, any vice, just roll the dice. I was handed cocaine. The winter soldier is a formidable ally, but on the sly, it can be a covert sleuth also. Ooo' lord whyyyy! Well, anyhow, I am jumping ahead of the narrative. Nothing is comparable to the hurt I felt with the exile from my father. As I matured, I realised the ordeal I was suffused in - it was too late. Olympia had begun to fall, the apple crumble fit for a king to devour. Insecurity plagued me. I no longer had confidence to quip, or joke with my peers. I was an outcast, a leper vagabonding amongst prudish children," Eric's complexion glistened with verve, "That felt incredible to unbosom - my priest, whom I strive to be shrove by."

Eric's dialect had been transfigured into romantic poetry, a Coleridge poem, superb in its lucidity, though masking its classical allusions seamlessly. The rhyme of an ancient mourner. He was now the Overlook's new curator.

Friedrich: "I am genuinely besotted with your honesty," Friedrich ascertained he must be in league with his romanticist, lest he be reprimanded for his prosaicism, "You are digging into your untraveled repressions."

Eric knew he was gaining the bridle of not only the room, but the audience, too, which were joyed by his performance thus far. Appeasing to the aspersive cynicism.

Friedrich was admiring his discipline in laboursome drudgery. Eric was eager to notice this, however, his unbelief in himself, led him to view the admiration as quite the contrary.

Start heralding the news, Eric has a neoteric muse. No longer under the serpent's constriction. He was ready to depart today, to fly away. His brain's way of thinking had been rewired. His systematic nervosity is now a metropolis that never slumbers. Ooo New York, New York, how he longed to laud the champagne cork apart. Effervescing the elate froth of spuming reckoning. A celebration was in arrears. The expectant mother vanquishing her travail, her Notre Dame womb let the water flow in fever down the river of pretty deities.

Friedrich: "I am going to ask you about your days at university; how did you find yourself wrapped in an excessive lifestyle, and how did the lady in white get a hold of you?"

Eric called upon the subfusc ghouls that lurked in his attic. He knew what begot this series of misadventures.

Eric: "I had been confined to a lock with no key, in desperation, beseeching for the warden to unfasten it. My feelings became sinister as I evolved older and a steadfast outcast, I was estranged to others. It led me to a conclusion. To friend comrades, I must prostitute to surfeiting in alcohol, or whatsoever, and ride the nacreous mayoress," as the remembrances surged Eric, his eyes twinkled a candlelit lust, "I had been down so goddamn long, debauch looked like heaven to me. A mere hiccup perplexed me. A hiccup was now a breath, a breath was now a burp, a burp was now a toxic excretion from my derrière.

"I wanted to be set free, like a bird in a tree that never had the tiniest bit of glee. Therefore, I drove myself down to a town, L.A, and with purpose chose my university to be located there. It was the home of excess, sex, drugs, and rock and roll. My acquaintance Ian and I, a couple of blockheads, excelled in our studies, and moved from the UK to L.A. Upon arrival, we instantly smelt the damp, moist, and fickle miasma of dissolution. It stank of ribald. It stenched beguiling for two simpletons.

"We both made a blood oath, we took a whetted blade, and vivisected our DNA in half. Our hands conjoined, and for a solemn second, we were familiarised, and not foreign, not extraterrestrial. We felt admired here—two deplorable Brits abroad, working hard to maintain a sustainable degree for their miserable career. Mr Mojo's rising. Mr Mojo awoke from his long-awaited usurp. The French Revolution, off with his head, let them eat bread. I can still recall my first session with the ivory detergent. It was a dismal day of leaden inclemency; however, the sun was somehow shining, Bob

Marley was wailing out of some radio, and Ian nestled upon my bed.

"He declared that to become the coolest of the bunch, we must munch this for lunch. I did as I was told; I was always a prudent student, never wicked. Henceforth this was the end, the doors had been unbolted. The wasp stung me, the enormous beat had riddled its ultimate rhyme. The desolation from my father's departure vanquished. I was lost in rancorous paradise, lost in the seven stages of hell, and stuck with several layers of additional grief. Mr Grim reaped for my mental stability. I would slither out of my torpor; I could not even retain my own mother's phone number. Ring, ring, that lashed her with a terrific sting. A chip on the old arthritic shoulder. Abraham subdued under a steel boulder.

"In the course of sybaritism, I encountered the petite girl of my dreams; she was zoomorphic. She belonged in an exotic menagerie, where people would queue to glimpse at her. We were gorillas on the dance floor, pixieish chimps amidst droll slaves. She understood my predicament, and my unceasing need to evacuate from banality."

Friedrich was in awe; this tale was rolling off the tip of his mind so smoothly, with no deceit and, yes, a loquacious exaggeration from his poetic dialect was issuing, but that is no crime. His chime was providing an asylum of solace; this problem could perhaps, be rested to lull, if he kept up these meritorious A stars. His whilom scars and his blemishes dissipated, vanished sans a trace. This crawling king snake was able to shake his lesions off; abrasions were fleeted abaft.

Eric: "My wife and I continued our unremitting love for Snow White for years and years. She awoke from her 100-year slumber, whereas I did not. She had gentrified her act.

We both quarrelled and quarrelled. Dispute after dispute, we failed to relate in any manner whatsoever, despite children being in the beggarly picture; of which we had two, after the first 3 years together. Patti and Camus are odd names, I know. But two odd peas in a singular pod tends to miscreate a freakish nightmare of a show, and this, trust me, I know. She was such a hypocrite: during her plight with pregnancy, she did not give up her snowdozing, the motor was still stirred. A live wire prepared to incite nocturnal aright.

"Our conflict began from there. I demanded she forswear her addiction, alas, she denied my docile request. The child came out malformed, diseased, and incurable. It was then that she reproved her vices, even sugar. Afterwards, with the impudence of a harlot, she enjoined that I follow suit. I declined her conquest, I politely declined, of course. We fought, fought, and brawled; it became a hyacinth house of phantasmic dread. A morgue of marital horrors. With the second pregnancy, our predicament worsened as intolerable. We no longer were forbidden fruit; our apple's soured; decay ran through the walls and up along the mountainous ceilings. In spite of all this I pledge on my grinning chin that I never laid a fin on her, or my next of kin. SO DO NOT DARE MISCLAIM, I LOVED HER MADLY, I ADORED HER SADLY! If I could only kiss her one fin…"

His metal plate commenced writing and roiling, yearning and burning, howling and scowling him—bang bang bang, the sadist cometh. Sticks and stones may break your bones, but metal plates shake your stable hormones askew. Interpret this as a figure of hyperbole, for he did not have a veritable metal plate corroding him, instead, a megrim ired such sempiternal fervour. A furious lion in its disconsolate cage.

Unchain the creature, it belongeth elsewhere. Who do you love? It can be aggrieving to waive away the one you so worship. Necessity is, nonetheless, the superlative entity.

Friedrich perceived these inconsolable smarts, and pronounced that they ought to call it an objectionable night, notwithstanding their still being time on his pendulum. They would meet again a week from today, at the peak of sunrise, when the moon has just consummated its diurnal ascendence. Nothing would intervene with a compromise. A crescent fool sought his muppet of a puppet.

This was to be their concluding chapter, the final film in the trilogy, albeit we hope it ends not like most trilogies. They always slacken their grasp of a dazzling narrative, and what propagated there to be a third in the franchise. Farewell, my fair mice and men.

Act 3

Here we are perceiving a man's quest through the conceptual and spiritual nostrum, differing from Marvin Gaye's methodology. The Church of Scientology is nowhere to be found. Nous voyons un voyage voyage, son esprit revient finalement. Let us hope this tale is resolved with a happy termination. I cannot bear more negativity, therefore, let us appoint positivity as dominion. There is a place called Kokomo, that is where you the dead are said to go, as means of succouring themselves from the infinite disappointments on Earth. No one dares blame you for your impermissible sins. We shall hebetate this fairytale of amiable gloom, for it needeth its beauty to sleep. Come with me, if you desire to live, my infants.

Our lugubrious jester, Eric, fortified himself with his blue suede shoes, and walked the talk towards his vehicle. No longer plundered by noxious despondency. No tears for fears remained, the first session had riven apart his inoperative scars, and the second had doused the fire from its purblind choler, and well - the third time is always the charm. Therapy is no exception to the couth. A man who is daunted by suffering is already suffering what he daunts. This had long been his maxim, his life's aphorism. Now he had deviated afar, like a butterfly shedding its chrysalid, and the little tweet twit birdie was all grown up. Such a prepossessing wonderment seeing your heretofore foetus transcend to a handsome man, or a beautiful woman. Neither should be discounted. Eric's grievances were set to soar off through an empyrean tinctured by a brilliant rainbow —a life he had been repining for was materialising —a life he felt the man up in the heavens had been dangling, and taunting him with, as if a spoilt child reaping his downtrodden avarice.

Our metamorph was venturing to read the classical emotions pertaining to mundane existence, and to bid his sorrow a good morrow. His sentiments could translate into a dandy fellow, he had often resided in inebriating auburn brandy with the morn, whilst drowning his joyous lorn. His wife evinced that etch men do not plain tears of woe, but sow their seeds of fruitage in Bordeaux. Allez les bleus! Men should not cry, a true man ought to erect tall, and tie any wants to defunct away. To be seen, not heard, as the wise olden Victorians quoted. Victoria knew best. Now this crawling king snake was able to shake his lesions off; abrasions fritter in an instant. Just add water, the mental label stated. Cathartic immolation - a contention debated since the Greeks, some say since the Neanderthals, in my prejudiced opinion, the whole balderdash deserved being expunged. With that hindsight, we are to dine on a banquet of Eric's soulful kitchen, let us ensue:

Eric knocked a singular toll upon the door, and was greeted by his shorn and graceful counsellor.

Eric: "Well, well, hello Friedrich, how are we on this stupendous day?" the oxymoron (since wan clouds fertilised the skies) unbefitting Eric's caustic humour, and defiling of hilarity.

Though Friedrich's erudition was severely bewildered by his audacity, he did not permit it to taint their opportune day. Friedrich had a fast distaste for Eric, he knew there was more than met the eye; a privy which loomed headward with Delphic animosity, as of a Sphynx prostrating itself. Yes, he was timorous, however, something awry stirred beneath the gladsome semblance; a door had not yet been unhinged. A key had not yet unlocked the song to his twisted phantasies.

Friedrich: "Superb, Eric. Thank you," he was unaffected by reciprocating with a successive jocularity, "Come in, the usual teapot rests in our midst. How are you feeling for today's session?"

Eric: "Excellent - I have been anticipating it all week, so enough with the parley, let's dive right into my swamp of emotions," as he voiced so, he boasted and flaunted his affairs amidst Friedrich's property. The regal arrogance mushroomed with a fungal hideosity.

They both sat opposite one another, and a gleam was apparent in both students' pupils. They were so tumefied that their irises appeared intoxicated on oldfangled ecstasy. Eric hallucinated that he was as suave as a twentieth-century fox, prancing around the extremities of the chamber. He thought him to be critically acclaimed, a five-star Broadway play, Truman Capote in all his flamboyance. I would rather not share a plate of breakfast with this flowery Tiffany; no amount of jewellery could dissuade me otherwise.

Friedrich: "I am sorry to bring up bygones, but I must demand we converse on where we impromptu ended. You began to be enraged, and became incredibly defensive over some incident with your ex-wife," a dilution of his right monocle, exemplifying his fiery intrigue, "What did you mean by this?"

Eric's knight in scintillant armour ruined upon Earth. The shooting star's Hollywood persona diminished into tenuous air. Dynamo had lost his sorcerous manoeuvrings to gull suspicions; however, as with any infamous eidolon, Eric attenuated his rapidity to yield to his fury, and looked as tranquil as possible.

Eric: "We wrangled a lot, which is wont with most marriages. Often over infructuous matters, and resulting in us disputing through querulous tempests. They were so outrageous, that, on occasion, our neighbours would frequent us, and query if anything was wrong. Hence, to evade this discomfiting air, I evacuate the house so as to assuage the turbulence inside my head. Incautiously, I succumbed to whiskey bars as my sanctum of sojourn and confided in their purports. They gave me closure and composure; the father above performed some miracle that kept me inside them, despite me scrupling over their ill repute. Then, the day afterwards, we would surpass the quarrel of yestereve, with a delirium of an all the more uproarious sort. Since she proceeded by castigating me for my degradation of the previous night. I was a shitty husband; that is the end of it. The end. Let's move onto something else."

Friedrich: "I am afraid it would be foolish to stop here, though we can discuss...yes, the whiskey bars - how did they transpire? If it is too painful, do you have any fond memories of them?"

Friedrich had kindled Eric's fire, the reveries of lurid intemperance flushed. Rushed through his organs, pumping sanguine up and down, all around his beloved crown. The clock was ticking, frail ice was thawing, upon which he threaded along. The Cirque du Soleil was about to perform their marvellous spectacle - the grand finale. How do I know? Have faith in me on this one, comrades. Mon copain se réveille. Eric spoke with complete purpose, every word counted, and he annihilated the punitive ambivalence.

Eric: "My friend Lou and I would visitate. We had a whale of time—an orca of a time, actually," his ineptitude for jesting was incensing, "We would go and order but umber whiskey; in most cases, we would quaff three down the hatchet, then be shown the way to the next whiskey bar; for they abominated our clangorous laughter. I never brought my car; I suppose I had some sense left. That being said, I am quite the backdoor man, I never went nowhere sans a stratagem. Sometimes, I was tempted to stick the old joystick in another delightsome dame, fornicate with an unchaste doxy, yet I withheld my weapon by crystallising it in my underwear, it was, nonetheless, not fair. I recall myself clarifying, in our first session, if my memory serves plumb, that I am a man of morals, respecting fidelity."

Friedrich, though, took every Lilliputian phrase with a multitude of McDonald's briny French fries, and disbelieved the verity of this mutterance.

Friedrich: "I feel you are holding something back from me. I believe you to be no deceiver - a man of sincere gambling morals. May I ask whether the name Selena Murdha rings any chimes?"

A blatant, ignorant whisper was temporised by Eric. It was so opaquely evident that this was false assurance.

Eric: "I have never heard of that obscure name, what a surname, though! Why do you ask preposterous questions?"

Friedrich: "A mischievous fowl rumoured an ugly hearsay about you to me. They impugned that you knew her."

Eric: "Well, fowls' songs can often be misconstrued. You know how the Chinese whisper, nowadays. Not all is black and white, there are silvery gulfs out there."

Friedrich: "Yes, I suppose you could negotiate so. Similar to how you never laid a finger upon your duteous wife."

The peaceable milieu was possessed by cunning wiles. The entirety was paralysed as gaunt hearsay scandalised throughout, the apocalypse dawning upon them. Eric essayed to reconcile his misgivings, by leering at the frolicsome painting of heavenly mischief, alas, it no longer bloomed a solicitous thrall, instead, he was bequeathed drab dolour. He frowned in simultaneous dismay and effrontery. The caramel tea encouraged no abetment, either. A lonely miscreant in the midst of being arraigned by his therapist - how ludicrous to retrospect, that one enrols in modernistic confessions, so as to aid themselves, and not be impeached before a facsimile of Lord Justice. A panacea which incorporates both physiological and judiciary practises. With Eric's attempts at disabuse floundering, in addition to the malady of a swoon emerging, he assumed the oratory tone of demented politician. Deluding his responses behind a gauntlet of simmering chicanery.

This was no longer therapeutic, but a subtle battle of accusatory claims. Shame was being affixed to Macbeth's name. Tarnishing his headstone with malignant intent, with a rather depressive cadence. Neither were prepared to foreclose their virile fortitudes, in effect, they were going to dragoon this through, until the dreadful endmost.

Eric: "What are you insinuating, Friedrich? We are going beyond good, and into the realm of evil here."

Friedrich: "I am simply suggesting that I think you have had some challenges in your life, yet instead of making you a shell of a man, I think you took this anguish, and like a false prophet, issued your wrath on the ones you loved."

Eric: "Are you now implying that I harmed my children? You used a plural there," empurpling with belligerence, "go on, tell me, what do you speculate I did?!!"

Friedrich: "I know what you have done, you play a game of charades with me, but shade cannot withstand flashlights: it reveals the candour adumbrating your diabolical moor."

Both poets were being arcane, but, alas, like a magnifying glass, both were delving underneath their egotistical psyches. Eric was in arrant denial, though there was no factual proof, it was circumstantial conjectures.

Eric: "I never laid a hand on them, nor my wife. Let the dead rest in quietude, do not libel our love, which we once cherished so," Eric opined that he might be accusing him of adultery, therefore, he changed his ploys, "Yes, I betrayed her with the lady in white, although I never slept with this woman you speak of - this Selena."

Friedrich: "As I stated before, I accuse you not of your loyalty, but I mention women whose lives you ceased to exist!"

The paintings gasped in horror; the nymphs, imps, faeries were astonished by the execrable charge. A bold and base accusation stood unsteady, nonetheless, Eric was ready for such an acute jab.

Eric: "Whatever you accuse me of, I have no clue, I would never hurt a fly."

This was a pocket rife with an enormous lie. My readers, you and I know it; for Christ's sake even Stephen King's Kurt Barlow knew it. Friedrich had sufficed with being misguided down Eric's holt of fallacies. He deduced it was time to regress Eric's faltering masculinity, and pounce upon this apposite caprice.

Friedrich: "All right, allow me to disentomb some names from the nether, in order to refresh your memory: Marilyn Hepburn, Audrey Day, Grace Novak, and lest we forget Elizabeth Mansfield."

With the mention of that last name, the malapert jaw on his African sculpture flung ajar, and the doorbell kneeled with bellows of protestations. Elizabeth Mansfield had been quartered and lynched in Times Square for all to be appaled at; her vaginal bowels had been pared into fashionable commodities. Her calves were handbags, her bosoms were implants, and her arms as disgustful footwear. It had caused a furore for the safety of the world's population; who wanted to inbreathe fresh air whilst sadists, like so, were walking the Earth, constantly unhinging the scheme of things.

Eric: "These are adventurous statements: you accuse me of cannibalistic, debauched, perverted, and offensive crimes against humanity, this relates not even to being abusive to one's nuptial partner. I no longer care about the false accusations of beating my spouse. This had been worldwide headlines, all over the TVC15. What fruit of concrete evidence have you, or what leads you to this ludicrous conclusion?"

Friedrich knew he must keep his theatrics up a little further, if he was to unsheathe deeper, he needed accountability. The drums could not roll without coercive surrender.

Friedrich: "Admitting is the first step to forgetting, a rule we therapists live by." with a haughty superiority.

Eric: "Screw your therapist's epigrams!" yowling as he felt the bludgeons of his past flagellate him, "You slander what is left of my righteous name."

Friedrich: "You never had a righteous name, nor did you ever have a name. Your name is not Eric, you can hide, but deceit always leaves a receipt."

Eric was threatened from this eldritch minacity. He knew he had been cornered, it was either fight or flight. He chose flight, he chose lust for life. What a wonderful repulse! He darted towards the door handle, and upon opening it, four men besuited in thick black, each with a silken tie, the finest of leather boots (polished and denuded to their bare arse), and their aforesaid suits befitting winsomely—not too tight, nor were they too loose; nighing on the masculine sophistication of a handshake, identical regulations apply here. The men in black hurled Eric back onto his appointed seat, and thronged him, as if a swarm of wraiths regrouping at their fallen brethren's interment. Eric recoiled to Friedrich, who peered into his damnable soul. Something ghostly was occurring, this was no sweet sixteen, no teen's vulgarly superfluous party, nothing hearty was taking place. Eric mused that the whole human race was against him. All four men in black spoke, through the use of brazen insouciance, in synchrony.

Men in black: "We are here to arrest you, Wayne, you have evaded the law for the last time. We have surveilled you, we know when you are aslumber, what you dream of at night, and how you take your tea down to a tea," they cackled in Luciferian emphasis.

There was no reason to hide or beguile himself anymore. They even knew his forename; the delusion was annulled. When a man meets his maker, he must shake her hand and rejoice, for his voice has been undyingly muted. He favoured being the passenger, nevertheless, he chose to ride through their cities' backsides, to ride the scrofulous waves from the Pacific's violent tides. He let the four men do the vilifying, men knew best from all the rest.

Men in black: "You are ill of the mind. You have syphilis upstairs. We know you did not philander with a consensual maid, nor did you wench with coquettes, but worse still, you took that anguish you wished to bestow upon your wife, and murdered countless helpless women. And Lou, you fool, he resented and repented for his iniquities - he came clean. He himself went to therapy to try to reckon with himself, albeit it inveigled him to avow to us his villainous crimes. It opened his pineal eye, and no longer did he regard his heinous acts as right. He no longer saw fulgid stars in the beauteous welkin, instead, he was harrowed by the macabre countenances of the innocent women you bestialised together.

"Moreover, shall we speak of your wife and kids? Were they suspicious of their deaths? When did she begin suspecting you?"

Eric, or with his pseudonym now dismantled, Wayne veered his advertency to the garden of celestial desires, and beheld it distort with aversion towards him, rescinding its potent dint of providing preternatural divinations by grimacing the direst of daymares at Wayne. He shuddered in consternation, and relented his fantastical rebuttals of his awful errancies against felines.

Wayne: "She began suspecting me from the third woman in, I once came back with carnage oozing onto my suede boots. I was foolish, heedless, and reckless, I admit. We fought more vehemently than ever before, as she condemned me for my atrocities, but it was the nose powder who was liable for these atrocities, I swear," redoubling his fawning supplications, "I SWEAR... I have since changed!!"

Friedrich: "You foul fuck, tell us what you did to your kids and wife—you are rampant with perversions."

Wayne paused, he had long eradicated that these acts were committed by him. He receded the narcotic blows when his mother perished, and thenceforth his remembrances warped into phantasmagoria. His former addiction, his former life long forgotten, fudged aslant like that of ancient vinyl. Melodic tunes that were no longer veristic in their audibility, nor were they legible, rendered both senses idle.

Wayne: "One day, I returned home, she had seen the news of my last, and final victim, save for my family. She had seen the terrifying mutilation botching upon Mansfield, and scorned and scolded me with ireful contempt. Screeching like a penitent harpy. Her octave range was incredible. I skulked into the kitchen, and since our country permits it, whilst she danced her last dance, I prised the magnum next to our cutlery drawer, and endorsed her with a single bullet to the heart. She now danced with death himself. I lapsed into a gay hysteria, and retrieved my soporific substances, inhaled a jolly breath of impure snow, and walked up the stairs, with very little concern. My face went an ominous blue. I saw my two babies one concluding time, one culminating time. I proceeded to smother them," Wayne bewailed through a fictitious sorrow, "I shot the sheriff, fine, you caught me, arrest me," he extended his arms, as a means of substantiating his surrender.

For the first instance in Wayne's pitiful existence, he had uncovered meaning, he had been truthful. There was no room to lie, for it was a malediction to live, and a benison to die. He was soon to become a whoreson in a menagerie, pinioned in an inconsiderate bane as his form of expiating him, or perhaps if the jury felt him culpable enough, racking him along the ecstatic chair.

Men in black: "Come with us, Wayne Shipman. Let us sail into unconsciousness."

With these words, he had given them his word on a wing. He had given his bluebird of life a fling, and made a mooncalf of himself. The golden years were up. For those discombobulated, a while ago, Lou had been maddened by contrition for his sins, the four men in black had coaxed him unawares into atoning; he now refrains from walking a hideous line. He no longer wanted to be the neighbourhood threat. He wished not to incite fret. When one contextualises these quizzical occurrences, they were frequenting a priest, where they confessed in slow though swift earnest. The priest, however, could not absolve Lou of his treacherous crimes, and thus, called the boys in blue, who, then, determined this to be a code red and alarmed their superiors: the men in black.

Wayne had since changed his name to Eric. Once the passing of his wife transpired, he felt the pressure dropping upon his conscience. Lighting McQueen's exhaust ran dry. They knew he, too, would acquiesce under strenuous pressure and wish to speak to someone of his malefactions against humanities. And this is where Friedrich came into the algebra equation. Sin minus tan equates to cause and effect. It is safe to say Wayne was peccant; he had his infantile misfortunes of patriarchal bereavement, yet never resolved them, and they soon expedited to afflicting other bystanders, as if poisoned by malarial evil. He let wrath take the pinnacle train of his invidious thought. He fought hard for many years to suppress the melancholy from his childhood— the bullying, the teasing, the father who was never truly present—but maleficence reined his bridle.

He had lived with his jumping jack flash cruise through studies, then along came Polly, which entailed folly through the guise of his addiction. He had critiqued his father's own alcoholism, though staggered aground towards blowing the ivory candle out morn and eve. Hypocrisy is inherited through one's family. His foot had been speeding with too much haste, operating on the grim peddle. Gas is inevitably depleted, as with a star burning out, and soon the char is no longer blistering.

I suppose, if we are to reflect in the mirror of the Wicked Queen, we must query so:

Mirror, mirror, upon that mighty wall, should we chastise them all? Mirror, mirror, who is enviously tall, should we call upon our own pangs, and envenom others with a maul? A brawl to the death, the voodoo doll injects them with baby's breath.

Until we meet again, my friends and foes, adios amigos.

The Man from Mars

Addiction comes in many different, indiscriminate convictions. For some, it is their chalice of red wine, irresistible when dining. For some, it is a blow from the fair snow queen. For some, a needle seeping infective tar. A scarcity of persons consider food to escalate to an addiction, but it is not hitherto that we have ascertained a crisis on our glum hands. Obesity is rife, and America strives to showcase the totalitarian regime of sugar. Commercialised to its saccharine galore. Big brother surveys their calorie intake, "Drink your diurnal milkshake!" Sometimes, I look upon our grand plot of land, and wish I was never truly begot at all.

Johnny was an American plus-size model, a corpulent flatulence which reverberated hedonistic crapulence. I behold an enormous silhouette of a man, with a pompous arse trailing in his circuitous wake, as if a remiss mannequin wading across her complacent stage. Let us harken back to Johnny's advent, when he had not yet sipped a fizzy pop, or indulged in some exquisite dark chocolate. His mother and father, though strict Mormons, knew not how to enforce legislation upon their child. They abhorred canting regulations to their Johnny, and, rather, took the approach of voluptuous excess as something deserving of appraisal, as if worshippers of

Epicurus. He, therefore, mushroomed fast, a seventies punk rocker, sturdily swaying his sloppy way through serious commitments.

At the age of two, he imbibed his primal can of Fanta, the indisputable god of all beverages. This is where it all derived from: to thank the Coca Cola Company for their great service to our nation's crisis. In dreams, he sat in Creams, ingurgitating on a maple syrup, banoffee toffee bananas, and Nutella spunkel-dust waffles. The contemporaneous cocktail is an elixir for tremors ahoy! All aboard Captain Crunch's luncheon as we set sail astride turbulent granules of artifice. When he reached the age of six, his mind flitted to idiotic folly, since the grinding tectonic neurons in his cranial region paled. The hemicranias stormed his faculties, and bastardised the ordinary precocity a child his age ought to evince, and possess, alas, the influx surging him neutered the fortuity of rathe-ripe intellect - let alone simplistic intelligence.

Attaining the demurral of eight, his daily weight-watching plan consisted of the following:

Breakfast: Two pounds of turkey bacon, two plethoras of swinish bacon convalescing amidst grease, and two pieces of French toast cooked in lard, instead of butter. Butter was too health-fastidious, hankered for a more desirable stone, a semi-precious stone was not enough for Johnny. To conclude, a large soda pop to ferment it all down.

A noontide snack: A bowl of extremely concentrated coco pops, bathed in his milk of choice, which was a salted caramel chocolate milk, and another large soda pop, a replica of ingredients of course, with all the added preservatives.

Luncheon: This is where we see the vastitude of our cookie monster in all his repulsory glutton. A steak seared in goose fat, moistening the beefy fries beside it, and alongside came a Five Guys Reese's pieces milkshake to further ail him.

An afternoon snack: A nimiety of buffalo chicken wings, covered in melted viscous cows' excretion, milking straight from the udder.

Dinner: Last but certainly not least, his mother would weigh a whole cow foetus on the scale, then proceed to castrate it before soused it in Fanta. She claimed it allowed les jus to ebb and tide. A songbird, a harmony of flavours, a symphony to the uncouth senses. This was annexed by his first vegetable mentioned thus far. Potatoes, however, are no vegetables, my nearests and dearests. Cauliflower cheese, fouled in mucoid unguent, personating the fluidity of coital lubricants, paired with some stilton, to get the gourmands raving and ranting. Needless to say, he terminated this with his final soda pop, one last firework before he slumbered in hay.

One must remember his age, this was but at the meagre age of eight. His weight scaled upwards, Simone Moro gliding with such elegant ease, such untimely sleaze. He must have had a psychotic break, as his strides were that of Conrad Anker, mooring himself with his dependable and comestible anchor up to the peak, the crest of the nacreous moon. His ceaseless honeymoon with glut and glut; their desires ingratiating higher and higher till they blazed like a squally fire. He signed, sealed, and delivered his life aspirations. He had no regrets. No contractions or qualms of character, on the contrary, he relished being the corporeal embodiment of avoirdupois.

Johnny's parental figures, overshadowed by their book of Mormon, or Morons - I lapse upon which of the two is correct, nonetheless, excuse my malapropism, I have an awful habit of muddling my diction into fiction - viewed their rancid son as none other than the deiform of Beltheim. Lady Madonna, his beloved mother, saw pure goodness in his sack of rolls. His father was slightly more concerned, nevertheless, too fearful of upsetting his mother's wishes, he left it be. Let bygones be bygones, aye?

He now attained the title of being a teen. Johnny was fourteen. His educational occupation foresaw the demise ahead. He refused to touch his school lunch, instead, voting for President Sugar's selection. All the while, in lieu of learning, he was yearning for an additional chocolate bar to satiate.

Johnny had reached Mount Logan, an impressive 5.959m above maritime rise. The air is thin, unlike his grim, miniscule waist. He could have been a rock-and-roll quasar glittering amongst mythic beatitude, alack, he chose his current pathetic inaptitude. His locks were as greasy as the pile of cagar upon his regal plate. The silver platter of unholy matter. His teachers were affected by his grotesque appearance, and atrocious impolitesse withal, the wooden chair could not even support his rotund carapace, bloating like a balloon aerated aplomb.

Crabs leave their decaying shells behind. Johnny needed to do so, lest he sought irreparable afflictions, but we humans are unable to compute such tasks. The computer, in short, refuses to calibrate such demands, it would rather reap the otiose reprimands. Our fellow Othello was becoming a stone, an immemorial monument. Frozen to stone, the moment he was shown. An electrical- eclectic light orchestra of pure revulsion. The peddle barbarised its lust upon the gas, baying to any naying, "Fuel ahoy, sugar for my boy!" The causticism revealed a morbid sinisterism.

He had now hit a standstill, a Shakespearean tragicomedy. Forget your midsummer life calvary, this was an unhumorous novice at work. He could no longer attend school, ergo, education was off the orthodox equator. A hot topic Johnny was. A fanciful beast from the east that never ceased to release its grip upon a sausage's roll. Exclusively Greggs, a man of insipid taste knew not of the steak bake being the sole decency they serve. The rest were all forgery at its finest.

With his morose torpidity scotching him there is no reason to further smoulder him. A career was out of sight. It was over, all over, 'tis all over, Miss Czechoslovona. Every day was an inclement day of tropical showers, albeit he found comfort in gulosity. Come rain or shine, so long as he had his greed, the fainéant perceived everything besides as a frivolous creed. A penchant had formed for caramelised Snickers, and Peanut M&Ms. Lest we omit a delightful Twirl, it made him dance his doldrums away. Terry's infrequent chocolate orange was his proclivity for a guilty pleasure. Jack's long-lost treasure.

Sugar speaks O' so suasory that it always demanded consent before it rent. A quick thrust of energetic connection. Is sugar not a modernist's drug? A streetcar named diabetes. Was there not a saviour to venge Johnny of his servitude? A man conceiving of a plan to unchain the hounds from their dreary frowns?

We now introduce Willy Wonka, who originated from Tennessee. His telephone rang one indolent day from a feverous incognito. It was Johnny's mother. She barked with all her irrational might, "O Mr Wonka, my son needeth to know the righteous path. He needeth someone to guideth, he has married a deceitful, sweet-talkin' woman. He has obtained the weight and height of Mount Chomo Lonzo, we require immediate and incumbent succour - otherwise I shall worry and worry for aye!" her vocality stuttered, and alarmed William with a salacious intrigue, deriving from his loathing of such sloths.

William, upon hearing this declaration of curiosity, decided it was right to haste down south to observe this attraction for himself. Chomo Lonzo is an impressive 7,804m wide. Across the border, he travelled, an illegal immigrant ambling great distances in his harlequin automobile, so as to shield this overripe oaf. Johnny was now an impressive twenty-five and gothically obese. A stunning flock of geese with flexuous locks of grease.

Wonka trespassed upon their domain, with an incommodious slither through their door, and spoke in candour, he was to charge them nothing for his utilities, he wished for the boy to but acknowledge his heedance with the utmost clearance, if a revival was what desiderated in his strive for survival. His father had left Johnny and his mother, since our former mention of his innominate clept. He could no longer stand the miasma of Johnny's sordid defecations. Wonka, a wily dietician, had yet to witness the supreme amorphia of suet incarnated. This was to be his primary perusal of a human, uglified by his ravenous avarice.

He strolled into the dorm, whilst conversing in niceties with Johnny's mother, and became baffled with febrile horror. O' dear god, the irreligious minotaur, the evil undead, all of the said had shed a tear. William spoke with melodious anger, in attempts to endow the exigent though kindly gravity of his ordeal.

"My God boy," said William, "I take my hat off to you, I hath never beheld such a buxom miscreation. You are in a worse strait than I had ever augured. Johnny, stop fooling amok, you better think of your terrific future. It is time you straighten right out, cut that toxin right out, reproof the sugar canes for you are nowt indebted. You are conjuring problems in this abode, and not just for yourself. For Christ's sake, blasphemed the sacrilegious William, from whom rage exudated, "Have you gawked at the mirror of late? If you did, you would notice that you look like the ghastliest chode to have lazed the Earth! Princess Crunchie would scowl at you, since you are unsightlier than a toad." William punctuated his contumely, by disarraying his delirium in transparency, hands aflame in the docile draught of Johnny's chamber.

The dietary prophet had malcontented his qualms, notwithstanding his words carried no weight. They were foiled and battered with immediacy, immersed down under with a monstrous cod into the profound fryer. People had told him time after time, if he continued to overgloom the scale, his tail would be seated in the infirmary. He, nonetheless, substantiated his conjectures to incline towards whatsoever solidified his ignorance. Why care for the jealous charlatans, envying to possess his ataraxia respecting unhealthful wonts. With this corroboration validated, the invalid infirmed his life the more, by redoubling his adventures astride pyretic cholesterol.

We now surmount the period of his sweet thirtieth, he commenced his banquet off with Snickers, an apple sour bitters, nocuous wastes, KitKat, Mars bars, Kinder Buenos, then for dessert (yes, that was but prefatory), he ate a whole live boar. The king of the feral jungle. A predator revered coming face-to-face with him. His chin had been long defunct and disnatured, the Reese's milkshakes had occasioned that. The spherical squares of sugar had erst pulverised his bone structure. He had now reached a whopping 8.611 in horizontal weight, as if a burly sun extending his candlelit fat outwards. The K2 Mountain had been attained. His body constantly strained. Immense pressure on a skeletal organism, he had long receded the art of arousing from his bed. In reality, the sole habit Johnny partook in was aural nonsense, blethering, blabbering and flabbering on about some fatuous crap. One day, the sunny side of his chancy yoke defiled. His fortune had heretofore balanced upon an airy stagnancy, though, sooner or later, his surfeits were bound to have afflicted him.

Humpy Dumpy headed down, his journey to the midst of the Earth was remarkable. He was the only one accountable. Gluttony is its own form of lechery. He could have studied to be a priest; he could have avoided rising up like a loaf of flyblown yeast. His salubrity declined, he was now in a sempiternal malady of eveneration, no magic nostrum could redeem him as an infamous rocketman, wretched Johnny. His putrescent liver shivered in continuance; even Elvis had not secured himself such fatty organs. His heart was the size of a ribeye steak, befitting for a zealous wolf. For indulgence's sake, his kidneys had mummified in lard. His intestines were as large as London's towering shard. His heart failed to palpitate his ichor to a sufficient extent throughout his system, leading to fatigue, and a nonplus of the brain. The dawn of the obese. Miss Candy had been so noxious, she let no other harmless nutrients approach him. Illnesses brewed within, his system could not barricade, since its brawn had dissipated; his metabolic arachnid had seethed down the waterspout. He bore a severe case of corrosive gout in his limbs. His mephitis reeked worse than a Swedish trout. His dole was doubtless heading for doom. To be just to Johnny his humour endured, for he nullified any anguishes, and was always jollified at his peril. An irksome persisted upon his countenance.

He had been warned through the virtue of endless letters, imploring for Johnny to prevent such indecent unravelling. Yet stubborn people will go down, like a captain and his keel, they must stay loyal to their newlyweds. His blood pressure faster than a commit rushing through the empyrean; Mars was reachable in the blink of an eye. The time machine. Stepping out, victory was far away, his arteries clogged with unlovely oil. Take my hand, Johnny. Come home, your time has been appointed.

Now we bear witness to his coronation.

The ceremony was one to behold, his viperish veins hissed, a ticking time bomb, compression. A 2001 Space Odyssey: O' Stanley, why did he need to be your protagonist? Gulliver's Travels met its cessation. His mother telephoned the ambulance, thereafter they rushed over with a crane to abet Johnny. They required metal storage units to even move the trencherman. The doctor entered, it was our fair Wonka, the sheen of melancholy hollowed his winsome eyes, his formless mouth, his beldame nose, and also his edged ears. Seldom had humanity sorrowed with such appalment.

It was raining droplets of crystallised diabetic lilts. The zodiac partisans would revel in such a marvel. The doctors foregathered, fearful of misdiagnosis. The big wheels were in motion, rejoicing at this edible phenomenon of surpassing natural bourns. They were apprehensive of stupefying our fellow under, nevertheless, it was a necessity.

During his somnolence, he dreamt of a garden of heavenly desires. Adam and Eve sang lullabies to Cane and Able. Able had since grown into a preacher, giving all the little infants a lick of his sugary lollipop. Cane now was a sugarholic, yet he brooked no consequences from his actions. Abraham sat by the lolling bush of fire, with his s'mores abreast. Mary propagated to a crispy M&M; not chocolate, nor peanut, they were impeached for their specific inclination. Jesus had been accused of devouring broccoli, a traitor to his mawkish kingdom, for this, the penance was good health and a lot of wealth. Johnny was cast out of his imaginary Garden of Eden extempore, with a roaring pain. A pain you do not just attain from a simple crack, or puny fracture. He awoke, and sensed the molestations throbbing from below decks.

He threw the duvet off; modesty was not needed. He no longer had legs. He attempted to feel these bereft limbs, and soon came to the hypothesis that he no longer had arms, either. He had always adored McDonald's false advertisements for their excuse of chicken nuggets, however, he had never wished to assimilate as one; alas, he had now transcended to what he had always devoured.

Poor Johnny had never quite accomplished his dream—to gross wider than Mount Everest—instead, he must hereafter spend the rest of his days in constant distress.

Nurture Over Nature

Man began with his Mother, a Matriarch gave birth to mankind. We Mandalorians sojourned as loyal, we Manchurians adhered to the simulative sport in our video game; we were the players submitting to her prayers. Then, one day, we turned, and the holocaust arose from the abyss, with vampiric maws, and therefore, inexorable to dismiss. Nature could no longer quash us at bay, and resulted in hiding amongst a pile of hay. Man was given all he needed, yet Darwin's theorem strove for progression, regression from our creator began. We masterfully crafted wonders, nevertheless, this sufficed not, for now we defy physical bourns, by mutating innocence to its converse. Have you ever rollicked with Dante in the waxen moonlight?

Let me put a pharos upon the direction we head.

In a future, not too far from our own realm, a man by the name of The Thin White Duke was venerated. He had built cities, sculptures, and, most of all, made renewable energy accessible to even the most beggared countries. Avarice hatched from its incubus, or, perchance, it always slept under the surface, nonetheless, it arose from an evil rapidity. Mankind's minds had been blown sixty-nine times already, however, they were not ready for such monstrosities. A cabinet of curiosities.

The Treaty of Versailles had been officiated, and Germany had been subdued into pitiable slavery anew. All that remained of them were their wits, locution, and expressionism. The Duke had been appointed as the rightful emperor, ruler, despot, over the state; they longed for money, and he had excessive amounts of it. The European Union's fear grew—a tumour needing to be removed, lest they a cardiovascular implosion combusts. The Thin White Duke lorded over Germany; the circumambient countries thought it wise to keep a keen eye upon the Duke, thus, they hired a laudable spy.

Along came our friend David, of innocent descent. His father was a sylvan farmer, travailing in the rich verdures of Nature's offspring, whereas his mother had no occupation. David strove for excellence, and was at the top of all his scholastic tasks. He never missed a singular lesson. Poor sod, he was Europe's dog, nothing but a servile hound. He had become a fairly accomplished detective, surpassing the expectations of countless, callous Chauvinists, who prejudiced his intelligence and faculties, since he originated from rural "nonsense". After much conferring, and in the end, concurring, the Masters of Covert offered him the métier of investigating the Duke's factories; naturally, he accepted such a feat of secrecy. I shall now leave you, the reader, to inspect these atrocities, and dissect the hideosities yonder. Let us go from the third-person - deserting your "unbiased" clairvoyant - to our first-person account of the tale.

3rd of September 2284, Tuesday.

I have arrived in the Germanic state, and I have been greeted with no contempt yet. They speak in a foreign tone, not German. This diction consists of symbolic rhythming and profane slurring, both synchronising as one. Their currency has plummeted: I can purchase myself a banquet, befitting that of a gluttonous king, for a meagre thousand shillings (the equivalent to five cents, comparative to the US's dollar terminology). My flat jitters me acold, something seems amiss, each wall I pass has the same frieze of paintings hung by a grizzly noose.

It is Goya's infamous Los Caprichos series. A peculiar, rather contrapuntal image for them to display, I must say.

They worship this slender and pale Duke; every sentence they utter finishes with "with kind regards to our fair Duke"; it baffles me. I am noticing that I am distancing myself from their cryptic, idyllic society. Nevertheless, my occupation at his notorious factory commences tomorrow at precisely 7pm - sharp. He disbelieves in early morning endeavouring, and favours the belief that the human vessel functions at its maximum capability at precisely 6pm onwards. I was informed he had attestations to substantiate such pseudo-science.

He is of the haughtier understanding that even educating children at 8am, is a concept no man should force upon their next of kin. I swear on my god-blessed chin that this "utopian" society has undertones of a rocky horror picture show. I have taken one of my mellow jellos (I fear, if I am overt in denouncing the narcotic, then they will apprehend me) tablets you have prescribed me. They have somewhat dulled my sorrows. Tomorrow marks a new dawn; my mission is to uncover the truth. And the truth is all I shall write in these letters to you.

4th of September 2284, Wednesday

I have made myself a comrade, John the Foreman, he is a man of their pagan church; he resides two rooms down in dorm x7x89. He hesitates with scepticism, avowing to me that a mutiny to this queer regime once rode on a white horse, albeit they were deracinated, and heralded as regicides of the direst sort. I have a few hours before I depart on my journey into the depths of industrious hell. In this factory, the more inquisitive I am to the populace around me, the more rage I seem to incite into their weak-willed hearts. I have never seen so many hearts jaundiced by cravenhood.

Stone cold ogles hit my soul, with each maudlin question I pose. I mean them no harm, but I fear in the depths of these walls, a murmurous talebearer lurks, waiting to relay my avid curiosity back to the Duke; he smirks, through the guise of nebulosity, and condescends his vindictive spite, relentlessly hammering them down until submissive.

I will write at a later time; now I must prepare myself for what lies ahead. I feel as if I am a child once more, about to recommence his affliction into the midst of imperious education.

I have returned from my shift, and I am content with my status in his industry. My sole operose errand is to heave around these titanium crates. I know not what sleeps within, though the workers are petrified of the merest stagger whilst carrying them. I almost cowped one, and worker 44vc-5 hurled obscene sentences, which I assumed were uncouth derogations. Their dialect cannot be German, they must have taken some DT classes, and malformed their own linguistics. One that simplifies language itself to its rudiments. I will venture to crack this DaVinci code within the due course.

The workers, or, rather, the populace, of facsimile Germany are wersh imbeciles. They cannot contain an inch, nor a centimetre of individualism, let alone an ordinary personality. They are impressionable serfs maundering their whiles away. It is as though I have walked into a group of nursery school children who have been castigated into a vacuous firmity. I will try to further converse with the population, by diversifying my thus far bland palette. I hunger to salten, or saccharify this sociable moonscape.

All I shall disclose is that at the end of today's toilsome, mind-mumbling-monotony, and tiresome shift, was that everyone in attendance had to chant their national anthem. Their national anthem was a mix of French and Italian, they appear to loathe their own ancestral culture. This is their anthem, I know not how they do not wrench their own earlobes out, from the smarting repetition of it:

"O bella ciao, bella ciao, bella ciao ciao ciao, contre nous de la tyrannie et vide nous de nos mémoires."

Its translation I am not plumb infused with surety since I was always impaired respecting mastering outlandish languages. What I surmise, from the little French I learnt in school, is that it mentions tyranny, however, it also juxtaposes so, by saying "rid them of their memories". Strange.

I shall keep these logs, they will become less and less frequent, and more intermittent. I shall purpose my information for crucial unearthing. I care not to send you nugatory balderdash, it will prove nothing, and not aid our cause. I have their version of "church" on Monday (I dare say I am excited for), this is when you will hear from me. Everyone must attend, therefore, if I am to subsume their unorthodox customs, I must concede to their wishes.

10th of September 2284, Tuesday

Last eve, I undertook the exquisite exercise of their monasteries. I forced myself to abide by their religious practices. The ceremony went as follows:

At precisely 2pm, on the demarcation, no later, no earlier, is when a droog arrived (these are their enslaved militia - The Duke's subversion of an army - clothed in a latex-purple uniform). He rang my doorbell, to be frank, I was unaware that the nightmarish abode had one. Upon unfastening and opening the gates to my safety, he spoke no words, he was dumb. He handed me the proper raiments for the ceremonial practices, and then debarked into a shadowy mist outside my cell. Inscribed on my parcel was the message: "made from the finest Ripstop nylon" - a ponderous choice of material for a religious habit. I suppose that is all the more reason why they are sacrilegious, instead.

The unfashionable composition consisted of a gangrenous green pair of trousers, befurbelowed by a chocolate diarrhoea shirt, alongside two bootless shoes that were stained with a yellow stitch on its seams. The outfit lacked any kind of coordination whatsoever. Thank the heathens, I was never one for being à la mode, nor prevailing an interest for the newfangled vogues. In my youth, I befriended a person named Marquis d' Etrangeté, who studied at Central St Martins, and if he saw me now, he would protest profusely at the sight of these miscreations. I, notwithstanding my animus, robed myself in my prayerful garments - ironed asymmetrically - and departed for the ethnic feast. I arrived, and clones after clones swabbed and populated the disarrayed streets. We were examined, by way of a swab test, performed before we were admitted our right of passage. You would think this medical idiosyncrasy to be probing for a viral infection, even a venereal virus, no, this was a test for "submissiveness", as they so flagrantly claimed. Complacency to the Duke's Legacy. The queue began to move in an octagonal circuit, inchmeal being shoved into the mute slums. The beloved shanty town, to meet our fair king and his jewelled crown. As I entered with trepidant nervosity, preceded by everyone else behind me, marching into the Colosseum; not a whisper or noise could be heard - absolute quietude. If a pencil was to drop, it would be as though America had once more irradiated a whole town, with its nuclear banes. I was imbued with the semblance of being a Kemetic prisoner, about to be mummified under regal pretences.

We sang our first hymn when the ominous clock struck precisely 5pm. I have seldom in my life felt such alienation; the diabolic hymn went so, if my recollection harkens in accuracy, though I must admit, I have been mislaying my memory of late:

"O' heavenly Duke, we worship your land
We are your band of gold!
You are our heartland!
Give us your hand, and let us drift away into your loving arms.
The people live in farms,
The children chime unremittingly

Our love for your thin skeletal beatitude
Forever devoted to your sincere and fair governing.
Let us sing in unity;
We are the community
We are One singular State,
We are all equal mates.
Our loving Benefactor,
The Duke who never puked on our white linen minds,
Be the kindest of men
His kiss blows in the belligerent winds without,
Five years appended to our just king.

He rules our next of kin,
Thus we must cling to him,
Our reverence for him is grand,
We have been infected,
Stung by the treacle of a bee's sting.

Bring us a chalice,
Filled with nowt of malice
And we shall wine and dine;
Christ's reincarnation lies in the fore,
Never shall we deplore for we adore!
Never shall He be concussed from our froward nonplus,
What does this make us?

We are his everlasting servants, surfeited by spirituous love."

Whilst this hymn was being intoned in disharmonious unity, my eyes darted around the room, flitting from one end to the other, like a surreptitious hawk. My heart was convulsing, I was in a delirious state. What have you, America, put me up against? Why am I your puppet? Though these zombified mummies are his unrequited swains, I fear you emulate his soporific maleficence. I am in the midst of relaxing, for recounting and reliving these oddities wakes me afright. My hand quivers as I write this. I am under immense, restrictive pressure, and gravity depresses me and contorts me.

I am perplexed at how he has wooed these men, women, and infants over. Roll over Beethoven, for this is the new monkey man in town. If they uncover me, I worry they will make my end as excruciating as possible, as a means of showing the world, "This is what happens when you mess with the Duke." Always a scowl when you are the anomaly amongst conformity. This starman makes me wonder: was it but his limitless riches that availed him to slip and slide through parliament, to initiate his ascendence to the throne? Did he need to murder a thousand crones, or more, to fulfil his destiny? Regardless, I had to vent to someone, since, with a paucity of confidants, I am waning adrift from sanity.

I shall resume with the churchy processions I witnessed, by ceasing my digression.

Here we were, muttering chants and hymns (if one can call them so) whilst having the Jesuite Feniute in our grand arms (their rendition of the "Bible") abreast everyone's hearts. I am a man who rejects any form of God, so this was of especial repugnance. It rent me to behold how far astray the gospel can be debauched from orthodoxy. Never in my life had I thought a Bible, let alone their poor rationalisation for one, would be cradled in my embraceful mitts. It gives me the shits even considering I did so. I apologise for my witty remarks, it is how I elevate the convulsing pressure in my cranium, inhuming inside me. It is as though something awry looms in the milieu they suspire, I suffered the ire of a painful migraine racking within, but nothing as horrid as this. The air was becoming a stifling baelfire of agony, when, like a fulgurating star from Uranus, the thin and fabled man crept from the shades into the limelight; and I must say, he gorgonized me, along with the other aesthetes surrounding me.

Startling in height, and though I watched from afar, his height was doubtless giant - Goliath even. Stupefying pallid eyes, as if riddled with bright nacres. His invariable pupils never strained nor blinked, they were agape twenty-four hours a day, and all night long they stood unvanquishable. His disquieting left hand was disgustedly scarred—I mean, hideously disfigured. It glared at you like a sore thumb amongst a curio of dwarfish fingers. I could not quite discern what and where the deformity derives from, all the same, I knew it was there. He flaunted it sans a singular scruple. He wore a bowler hat, its rim was silver, causing it to gleam, a brilliant beacon, a luminescent lighthouse. Alongside him were droogs, yet these outshone the one who had so impromptu interrupted my false privacy.

These were very slender though mesomorphic men, trees rather than men; he had ten who guarded him all the time. They could not have been human, they could not have been from the kingdom of animals, either. O' Lady Godiva, give me a heavenward sign. I need to know what these scapegraces are, and what their purpose is. My wits surmised that the star of this grotesquerie was the Duke. Blanche Debois would scamper aside for his lawless temper. The Duke from the west—how wizardly he walks. His voice dispelled from his gates with such taciturnity, he was not one for inutile formalities. Every sentence was measured, and weighed, before it was spoken aloud.

"My people," said the Duke, with an august hauteur, "my men and my women, thank you for coming. Though this may be mandatory, I commend you, and salute you for your honesty. Honesty is key to our survival, and to our honour.

"We are damned by other societies, other cities, other countries, and continents. Let this not distance you from our irreversible success.

"We are one, we are the suffragettes. Is that not correct?" Without a second of hesitation, everyone hurled him a devout "Yes, Duke, we are your kooks." I was not wise of this being an incumbent requisite of the ceremony, therefore, it sparked a sour cataclysm through the silent slaves. Indignation to my left and right. I declared I had a dreadful lurgy. They untethered their disrelish whereto the umbrage mollified.

We were allowed to depart at 7pm, everything rotated in prime numbers, a numerical way of living. We all marched out, our feet could be heard scouring the interior of the metallic-pathed floors; reverberating when pulverising its metal, and echoing throughout this canorous sarcophagus. I strolled back to my abode, my metal tin can of a dormitory. As I took my promenade, eyes pierced me hither and thither. People are O' so rebarbative when you're foreign. Faces cause such a fright, they instigate a fight or flight reaction. Children seem devilish when you're alone. Streets once constructed in perfect idyll, now ruined like a flower plundered by blight. No one remembers your name when you're another letter of the numeric alphabet. People are strange when you seem deranged.

I returned at around 8pm, since I opted for a longer route back, so as to tranquilise my feverish thoughts. I needed to establish some order. My mission is to unbury the primordial relics of filth on their Duke. I shall visit their library, adorned with unsettling gothicism and viperous gargoyles, in the successive days to see what information I can collate about their history. If they have not misconstrued it to their incoherent will, that is.

11th of September 2284, Wednesday

I strolled off this morning to the communal library, known to them as "The Knowledge of Chicanes". No old hag, as is wont in such literary havens, stood before me as the head librarian, rather a quizzical figure, a virid foetor pared her skin's colouration, dare I say its gender was 'non- binary', but, in truth, I could not categorise her, nor which plain she belonged to. It - to be crude - had the bosoms of a buxom woman, the facial whiskers of an unruly man, and the nose of a witchy female temptress, which was, then, contrasted by the chiselled cheekbone structure of an arrogant male. I had hitherto never seen such absurd, circumstantial characteristics.

It was an obscurity out of the Brothers Grimm's book of twisted yet magical fairytales. Her tone was not hostile, yet neither was it very endearing, or docile. I demanded to know where the historical section was, provoking her to press a rectangular button, which then lit a fulgurous passageway straight to the section I sought. A kaleidoscopic mystic led me through the tree to knowledge. I strode along in unchary euphoria, beguiled by their ingenuous pyrotechnics. I always enjoyed history; it was my second favourite study. My most beloved being English literature.

I had arrived at my destination. By Jehovah's witness, I had hit the motherload. In front of me lay more books than calcined during World War Two: the lolling flames of vellum, and commonplace pages, winnowing against the conflagrating fire. There were books as thickset as any ebon man's pizzle. I leafed, skinned, and devoured every morsel. Fascination fattened to corpulence, a rotund plum set to explode. Davy Jones had plunged his curse into my rapt spleen. I was what school bullies yowled as "a nerd", I was too eager for my own good. A psychotic killer, I felt like a real-life wire, my tyre depleting until arid with erudite luminosity. I had run a verse through their historical literature, overwrought with inquisitive thirst.

It seems all physical evidence of western dominance has been annihilated. The atom bomb marred, and the victors rejoiced at having begot an execrable bastard. According to the illegitimate antiquarians, the sole remaining "victors" on Earth were its despicable tyrants: eulogising Stalin, Hitler, Mussolini, and Franco for their nefarious malefactions. God save their gracious indignity. Why must they be predisposed to malignity? I had gathered from the banquet before me that their state was morally communist, yet its dogma resided in the foundations of fascism - some baseborn fled from normal society. At its head, this government was but another autocracy, another brick in the wall of dictatorships that have come and gone in our perennial time.

The only thoughts that ran through my taut veins were of a doleful sense of commiseration. The children of men were to be taught a false identity of their own country's history, and of previous atrocious beings. False prophets whose underbite stood so truculent that one could not help but stare, even if it was rude. Let candour be displayed nude, unveiled in a sheath of brooding clarity. The more I deigned through their vulgarity, the more disturbed my bilious stomach misstepped. The more I progressed, the deeper my nausea encompassed my every wakeful train of consternation.

The train tracks tilted askew, and yet they would not divert. Riffeting and pivoting vertigo descended me further and further. Their genesis story, from what I gathered in the tale titled "The Day The Tin Man Gave Birth", was another farcical anecdote of their incalculable cozenages. They counterfeited the quintessential fragments from the Bible, anteceding Adam and Eve's manifestations.

It went thus:

"On the first day, the Tin Man forged the Galactica.
On the second day, the Tin Man sparked electricity.
On the third day, the Tin Man kindled the blaze.
On the fourth day, the Tin Man maketh man.
On the fifth day, the Tin Man inspired a nation.
On the sixth day, the Tin Man frustrated the rebellion.

On the seventh, and Holiest Day, the Tin Man quashed the temptation to rest: rest is for sinners, and sinners must be terminated at once."

This version of Genesis and the Bible's interpretation of our fashioning, were tragic in their ludicrousy. This ruse, being fed into the minds of mouldable children alike, is a recipe for a pernicious disaster which must be prevented from arising. Children are vulnerable little faeries, ascribable to their inexperience in the realm of existence. They lack any sense of interpretation. Au fond, I fret these juvenile mice are gourmandising off the mildewy cheese, which is envenoming their perspectives. Where youthood proffers an outlook to broaden, theirs dwindled to an insular nescience. Percase, it might straiten to bigotry. I shall disentomb what my clandestines have been yearning for: the cultural tale of Adam and his faithful Eve. The peccant fornication which eventuated their banishment from paradise.

It ensued so:

"The Tin Man welded man with his machinery, he made him antithetical to his own imagination. Man deserved not to be blessed with such inarguable excellence. He appointed him King of the Physical Plain, and dubbed him 'The Thin White Duke'. The man was distressed for his fellow comrades, and with zeal, took it upon himself to craft a platonic companion. He felt that man required something to impregnate her, thus behoving her with a cavernous defect.

"It was a strenuous, exertive task, but with the succour of his never ceasing divinity, he willed a map for the infinitude of appearances she could be characterised by. He was not timorous about begifting her with a lecherous complexion. Hexing the female form into corporeality, with the help of the male gaze, and man's exorbitant insight into the feline psyche, he made "Lady McBits". The Duke, upon beholding her, was ravished by woolly lust. Infatuated with his waxen effigy. His hound dog howled for her puss in boots, nonetheless, the Tin Man gave his one commandment.

"The Tin Man: 'You shall not copulate, you shall neither thrust, nor combust in this beauteous nymph. If you do, I shall shun you both for eternity in a pit of celibacy.'

"The wise man solicited decrees, and decrees are to be followed. For seven long, laborious weeks, which felt like frigid winters eloped by despiteful seasons, they resisted the mere postulation of touching. Not even a simple hug was bestowed upon each other's velvet, tight yet supple skin.

"There would be no next of kin, no fornicating of another's shin. Then, on a star-crossed day, Lady McBits was bathing herself in the cobalt waters, when along came Polly. The Devil himself, in the shape of an absorbent female, pranced and swayed her jewels around the place, as if a wanton mace. It aroused an eroticism heretofore unconceived in our maid. It made her neglect her steadfast judgement, and controverted it, instead, by wagering how much the Duke would marvel at Polly's halcyon anatomy.

"Never had eyes averred such female dominance. She was to model herself on this woman. The disguised Devil gallanted towards her. He secreted within his ambidextrous sexe, he knew too well that the cinders of disobedience needed but a gentle push, and the derelict tower of Bethlehem would collapse. Then he or she whispered, 'Darling, darling, ohhh darling, we must evoke carnal deviance, and rebuke common morality. Feed these pieties to the lions!' These words were all it took to unbalance her obeisance. The devil had interlaced not any palpable, or physical malisons, his ingenuity domiciled in his aptitude for somatic suasion. He ingrained his gossamer by virtue of passive words. O' how forte language is, when utilised to its supernal fruition.

"Upon returning, and abutting the Duke in the midst of reveries, Lady McBits deflowered herself of her vestments, and ambushed the innocent Duke. Lady's svelte thighs laxed in a gainly curvature; her rubenesque breasts depended in midair, nestling at a uniform horizon of fleshly seduction; the darksome marine of hair flowed with serene elegance, halting below her sultry posterior; the sensuous allurement of its sybaritic sphericity; the ugly though comely visage effused droplets of glacé dew. The Duke was embalmed in an awesome furore of dread, and hankered for them to be wed. His eyes began to scintillate with crimson armour - a sight for wry eyes. His pupils were transfixed, they were looking into the fairest star of them all. She proceeded to stoop even farther from grace, by clenching his bawdy phallus.

"Before Lady McBits could nibble at this briny substance. The guileful Devil spurred in torrents of discomfiting milk. He had yet not acquired a perdurance, though, being respectful, this sensation was novel, and extraneous.

"Their reckoning, however, was to be allotted. No fallen soul can elude, or illude, the fatidic Tin Man.

"The Tin Man: 'My child, my dear lady, take your business elsewhere. I have no care for your begrudging, simpleton's crudity. I think you will find there will be a special place in Hades for you. Duke, my young foolish boy, I was a joker to think a mortal woman could live to your standard of morality, thus, she shall be banished for a thousand years, and when she returns, make her your unfaltering slave. If she disobeys once more, make her head concave for then she will behave. Put her on a leash, and saunter her wherever you go, I grant you this chateau as a means of displaying my condolence for my mistaken credence in anything besides Men.'

With these sage words, God proclaimed who was who. Whom was the dominant sex, and ergo cast a curse upon femininity."

It is probable you read this, and were mystified by such a tale. I mean, one must accredit it, since it truly is a memorable piece of literature. The Duke, or whosoever toils over these misrepresentations, possesses a frightful cunning; they could flex facts to their whim, as if devious swimmers parting the spurious seas with ease. An ancient relic of disgrace, now modernised to benefit these conspicuous minds. It seems I have a broken heart again, this crane has lifted such an unimaginable bane. I no longer wish to remain incognito; I wish to ascend the peak of the Duke's tower, and cry out to all below to descend from their indoctrinated beliefs. What is the price for your mute mouth? What is the price of your purblind eye? The vilest insolence in this libel was the idolatrous Duke elevating he and men beyond females. Maligning them with his factitious recounting of the Bible.

After this scurrility, I deduced the importance of delving deeper, therefore, I started perusing their dictionary, to see specific colloquialisms, or accents, they used in quotidian confabulations, which might sound alien to me - or us. I came across some intellectually interesting synonyms for our language. There appears to be an obsoletion of words such as "no", "decline", "stop", and "refuse". They have commingled these negative connotations, and personal choices, for a more apathetic approach. Whereas we favour a pleasanter decorum of rejection to an offer, if your desired answer is no. I have also struck gold, with what these slender shadows were during their terrific ceremony.

They are the "diamond dogs", as christened, a genetically bestialised race of synthetic humans. A superior version of his piteous slaves - the droogs - though, the irony being that both are slaves to his institute, if we are to philosophise. The diamond dogs are written in their literature as arthropods by birth, but infusing chemical sorcery, their blood is adulterated with that of a jaguar, giraffe, and chimp. These creatures detain anyone who opposes the Duke's law and disorder. From the images shown, they have the risible body of their ancestral giraffes, their jaguar's speed, and the brute strength of the chimp.

A sanguinary transfusion is what genetically enhances his witless subjects— our suppositions were correct, since genetic mutations must be shaded beneath the depths of this society. It is possible, too, that I have been as unobservant as a bat. The librarian herself was the strangest creature I had yet to come face-to-face with, however, whilst promenading around town, I have caught a glance at irregularities aplenty, and a range of unpretty monstrosities. From further reading, the punishment here is to be brought to the catacombs, and be 'rectified'. I assume rectifying means modifying, and disfiguring. I had seen enough, and took my leave of the premises. I had seen sufficient implicit messages.

Upon arriving back at my concave cell, I was bowling the kettle to make myself a tea when, in the corner of my spectacle, I saw a marvel. This whole time, I had a television. How had I not discerned this beforehand? I planned to scroll through their satellite of propaganda before hitting the hay for rest, in advance of another taxing day at the factory. I sifted through the visionary contraption, and as I had boded, it all hailed the righteous and due king, enthroning him through falsehoods. One propelled me into a state of hysteria: using the motif of a globular object, the presenter orating a prehistoric rhyme of some foreign mariner. The rhyme went as follows:

"Long live the Duke, Our rightful heir
Any who denies his love must face a good spook!
He is a breath of unpolluted air.
His name lights our fair city, like a bright vermillion flare.
Never a frown,
When his golden crown,
Sits aloft the Duke, but rebuke it, if the bearer be a clown!"

Baulking a few banal clicks through their satellite of drollery, I doused its stygian mirror. To be frank, even their blatant propaganda rivals ours across multiple shores. There is never anything to mindlessly drone off to nowadays. I uncovered all their networks to be buffoonery, jestering and haunting their cretinous idiocy at us, like a pair of bosomy titillations. Don't you wonder sometimes about the gift of sound and vision. All we do is sit and listen to our television. Does it tell the truth, or is it all one big vaudeville, being surveyed attentively by an innocuous sleuth? Not me, though, I assure you.

22nd of September 2284, Friday

I have been the busiest of bees since my last writing. I befriended my co-workers (the unfortunate met his grisly lot - you will see later on), they are a sapphire amongst repetitive paysans. Every other conversation, save his and mine, protracts to the extent of "how the weather is bitter and glacial". How British of them! I have noticed we are under constant surveillance, as if an umbrous brother looming over his younger sibling, under the severest instructions from his supercilious mother. Suffocating his people, with the droogs, whom the gloam engulfs and protects, in every corner of your field of view. Who knew anxiety could transpierce such an inanimate triviality. In spite of being spirited under by a poignant anchor, I am surprised to have risen in the ranks.

They now have the utmost confidence in my value to the factory. In the wasp factory, we are manufacturing substances unheard of to the naked eye. Unsung to the insentient poets of yesteryear. Myriads of these fabrications are purposed for warfare, or pseudo-science.

I have distinguished that if one steps out of line, or is too clement to himself, the penance is to be banished, shunned afar; where no glorious auroras dare bless. They towed away to the tomb of Tutankhamun, waiting for the raiders to plumage your goods for some flippant museum. As stated, before I digressed, I had made comrades with a fellow worker (his worker I.D. wa D-503, meaning he was of lowly class - he was not from the same apple tree as you or I). He had injured his spinal cord the previous day by lugging a leviathan cumber. Nevertheless, the show must go on, so when he was unable to dance to the cruelty of plum fairy's enjoins, he was held at border control, and the diamond dogs were ordained to punish him. Wretched D-503, he had inbreathed his final hour in this lustreless town. I pray he had a brisk extermination.

On Monday, I witnessed beauty. A rebellion transpired; The House of Commons must have sufficed with their subjugation. Rebel, rebel, they gleaned so brightly. Rebels, rebels made my blood cells curdle, as if I were rotten milk. It was time to expunge the androids who smothered the populace. I say all of this, as these were my hopes, my aspirations, and my ambitious futurity, but alas, nothing prevailed. Art least, nothing efficacious. The diamond dogs quenched the usurp by effacing them; the moon of ichor suffused upon us. Pest controls were called to action, with an air of electric relaxation, they emerged from a phantom mist and, with a handful of immense cannons wrecked their own, half-kindred compeers. You know manipulation is at play, when the military is disaffected by slaughtering the people they are hired to safeguard.

Once the entire revolution was frustrated, the leader of the uproar was brought forth. He was deposited in the midst of the avenue, and like a willow in the wind, the Duke up whirled from somewhere yonder reality. In his hands, lay a machine of mechanical origin. The crowd could have been an Edvard Munch painting, for complexions atrophied to a featureless pallor. Bemoaning and bemoaning; the sole ado you could hear were tears of etch fear. The heinous Duke was affronted alight with exasperation. How dare his people oppose him? How dare they shriek and snare their opinion of his governing? He strolled up to the treasonous leader, his disloyal and undevout underling, the only man who had the valour to gut his pride.

His glare spoke a thousand words, it was the look of "I shall mark you for murder, you will be the exemplar of what betides if you step out of line." His machine flung a nugatory pellet at him. I resisted the temptation to laugh. Within a nanosecond, however, he was undergoing transformation, a mutation, and a metamorphosis. Kafka had presaged these doles erst. The church would have called it a prophecy; in plain, I called it satanic.

His ears malformed to horns, his feet gnarled and spurted hooves, and his mouth elongated into some Loch Ness nightmare. His pupils dilated, and defaced viridescent. The man in front of us looked about to combust, he had been imprecated. As his transfiguration persisted, wings embowelled from his spine, with acute, eagle-like wings - wings, great big fucking things. The pale Duke beckoned the crowd to engird him, and encompassed by this mass mania, he spoke:

"If any of you venture to mime this abject shitshow anew, I will sunder the rations. None of you are assassins. None of you were born in Athens. Thus, heed my declaration: I do have admiration for this winter soldier, but like any gauche purloiner, he must be damned." with vocality gravitated the essence of hatred, and enmity. I daunted at this impermissible despot, and yet, I concur the sentiments which roil me aswoon, and covet to brave a scythe at his heart. I am not mad, though, since I know it would be in vain. Alas, if I could buttress cognate art against him, to then subdue him aground.

I returned "home" that crepuscule with a ghastly fright impugning from the preceding events, a flight of the Conchords awaiting my plight. When the time is apt, I shall gather my metaphorical sword (the recipients of this entry), and crush this egoist with his degenerate methods.

29th of September 2284, Friday

It seems today that all you see is violence and brutality. What happened to all the glee? Christmas is no longer merry. Drown your sorrow in a bottle of the finest cherry, for it might be your last. An eyrie is where my sanity reposes, beside a murder of crows—my sinistrous reality. Ah, the mirth of being a twentieth-century fox.

Pardon me, the intrusive thoughts, once more, chafe and scrape away at my lucidity. I am demented here!

Since I last wrote to you, my just fellows, the factory has experienced tremendous renovations, and upgraded its inventory. We have been demanded to increase our work rate. Saint Nicholas' enthralled elfins are up to their fortissimo ode, as we approach the crescendo. We are constructing some garish tawdry inaugurating a robotic cadaver as animate. I know not its purpose, nor its function; it is very recondite. I must say during the manufacturing, my mind pondered and drifted into the unconscious. I leered, spellbound, bemused by what my vision beheld. I wondered, how much metal could a metal machine meticulously mash, and how many skulls could it, therefore, bash?

We had a casualty on Tuesday. Someone was too preoccupied with their wallowing in mire, and ended up in their sepulchral pyre. He fell into the plenitude of scorching magma; we watched (everyone), as his carcass writhed akimbo, as if an orange whip flagellating to and fro. As his malaise was excruciating, he ere long eclipsed into the billow of vermeil ocean of coulee. The final image we had of him was his fossilised body dusked to obsidian.

His penultimate breaths were apparent, too, as they floated to the surface, lingering bubbles of regret rose to the surface as clear as dawn. For the reliquary of our shift, a miasmic epidermis reeked throughout. There is no stench as horrible as that of cremating flesh.

On Wednesday, I was walking on Rue Oberkampf, when I saw an art gallery that appeared to be open, and gratis. As one does, I changed the destination in my internal Sat Nav, and meandered within.

The paintings in attendance evidenced drear canvases, with little to no unique character. One, titled "Depression", embodied a caliginous wraith, misshapen and distorted, holding an aureate cup. The background was a bleak grey, and on the cup, peculiarly enough, the words "cold" were impressed. I suppose the connotation is up for interpretation, as with most art, if not all. One must catechise the subtle meaning of a painting - or, in actuality, what I am insinuating is - what envisionments are aroused from your perusal, and how does it acquit you of your monotony? Does it fit your sunlit conscience? Walls upon walls of decaying creativity is all I saw.

Forlorn blots of unctuous paint were extempore fawned across its body, and thrown onto the canvas. Barren wastelands, a putrescent helianthus. This, my friend, is the end. My only friend is now gone. I quitted with immediacy, dissatisfied with what I was dismayed by. Here, I was thinking this was to be suffragette city's point of redemption. They, after bootless corroboration, remain suffering martyrs in my mind.

Onto a more positive note, John the Foreman, now a shrewd accomplice of mine, has given me clever advice over the past few weeks. All his advice has succeeded in infiltrating their ranks. To him, I owe many thanks. I am now a corporal supervisor of mechanical operations. What this title means, is that I have absolutely no clue, either, nonetheless, I do know this is a satisfactory accrue to possess. I aim to shame them next, during work on the morrow, I wish to further assimilate into their loathly psyche. I shall press onwards with my reveal through my 17-minute break - a defamatory allowance of respite, however, it serves my intent just so. There is a door I can now access called "The Morgue". I will see what I can unclothe here, as though distautening the corset on a virginal demoiselle.

30th of September 2284, Saturday

If sleep is a virtue, it was a virtue I lacked last night. I tossed in a continuum on my roguish bed sheets, my malcontent teeth gurning, and my mind was wound up like a melancholy-go-round. Visceral, warm photographs of deathly doctorings flashed in my forepart. My qualms kept repassing, a broken cassette player pirouetting over the plastic film inside it. The curious incident with the changeful bird-man had not ceased to haunt me. Since its occurrence, every morning, with my artificial tea, I make a plea to myself to prevent these dark films that fetter on loop. Alas, I conjecture this is what I get for being a snoop, and for invading the secrecy of this freakish sanctum.

I now depart for a hard day's drudgery—another day of beaming along a tightrope, pertaining to the awes of le Cirque du Soleil. If I am to flounder, let them wrap a brail around my frail nape, and wring upwards, whilst my body convulses in suicidal illogicality. The miserable Pierrot has glowered enough, it is time to capitulate this bluff. It is like a jungle sometimes; it bewilders me to wonder how I keep on sinking under. How do my enzymes stay celibate, when all I see are indelible crimes? It makes me wonder how I blunder through these streets with cordiality amidst my private dolour. Well, the vengeful o'clock has struck. I shall excavate the covert Morgue, by exenterating the sordid bowels of the Duke's secretest privies. I shall paunch an evil stag, to then taxidermy its riddles to the public.

Bid me adieu, for I require the superlunary intervention of God himself.

I have returned, and I think I should be administered into a lunatic asylum, for no one wishes to live in the phylum of the Duke.

The unearthing happened with an insipid sky blearing. The unusual darkness of twilight hasting to reign supreme. Not much bestirred amidst the Germanic streets. I did, however, begin to hallucinate, by hearing birds which chirped the chant of the girdling skeletal family; their illusory wings swaying gangly hither and thither. The streets felt as elongated as ever before, never had I suffered such strenuous steps bemiring my will to perdure. Preconceptual existence stilled in the air; I inhaled insalubrious oxygen. Profound but shallow speculation aflutter, and sips aerating and inflated my courageous alveoli - an agley ally of mine. I must have belaboured harder than any bondslave in the history of the tyrannous trade, my hands in flames, my knee joints quibbed with an evident delusion of no cartilage remaining, and best we forget the soles of my slavish feet.

It was my way of feeling less contrite for the treachery I was about to pull out of my deck of cards. My 17-minute break arrived at full throttle. I knew that, with an invisible stopwatch, they calculated my every move, they timed each absent second, with hawkish vigilance. They were zealots to my wake. I slid past my assailants, and entered the room, entitled "The Morgue".

As I ingressed, a draught from the arctic swept me off my feet, a thick sleet inhibited my perlucid sight, and a snow-white left me nonplussed. I walked and walked, as if I had travelled the world in eighty days, yet during this cumbersome expedition, our keel, berthed in Antarctica, had been castigated into forfeiting our annual leave to Corsica. I flicked an archaic switch, besprinkling grim residua of dust at me, and several candles enlightened with flexuous flames, oscillating round and round. There were hundreds of headless heads, thousands of beds now lay without their amative lovers, pauperised mother's giving no druthers—choiceless—there would be no rejoicing, no voicing their grudges.

Each head had an aspect of individuality, an aspect of singularity, although they were drowned out by peculiarity. I sauntered into the unquiet chamber; my face hit by a loud thunderball at all this mutilative perfidy. Did his people know of these bestial valuables? Did they realise where the lepers were forsaken to vagabond? Could they have envisaged where their deceased slumbered, after an exquisite lifetime of smarts? And if they could, had they presumed it to be such a condemnable grotesquerie?

I saw a bookshelf, and knew from my experience of Agatha Christie novels that all tragedies have three acts to them. There would be some switch to deepen me farther into the pits of the Duke's Tophet. Nothing is ever as plain as meets the eye, everything is always slightly awry, nothing is as simple as A.B, and lest we omit C. I cared not for courtesy, thus, in a fit of monkeyish choler, I ravaged the shelves, throwing bananas, once a relic, now an extreme horror. I was a Wall Street hustler, on his way to con another credulous fool into purchasing penny stocks, flocks of idiots believing their world to be Elysian. The planet of the apes dawned.

My magic wand prevailed, and upon launching a book of scientific interest across the universe, the shelf morphed. Disparate to what you see in the factitious films, it was a lot less intriguing—quite dull, actually. What lurked behind, however, was beyond the bourns whereof any creative cerebrum can forge from their inner fallacies. The invention of fire was adust, comparative to this bedlamite of faith. Glass everywhere, cabinets of glaucous crystals, mosaics of tortuous prosaic closets. Intrigue sparked, my deal with the devil was to shovel the unutterable truth at you, my complicit audience.

I weaved my way into the palace, my appetite for the knowledge could no longer be suppressed, the anorexia had at last been quenched. I kept dead silent; not a word was to spoliate this sacred moment. I took one final glance behind me, and discerned that if I was to return through that door, I would soon succumb to curiosity. I needed to see what atrocity lay yonder. When a man confronts a surrealscape, when he is illumined to the path of the inquisitive man; he must stand his ground and endure compliance. Best to keep the client reliant on you. Hushing trepidation teethed in swift blows, enrapturing me hence. A noisome malodour of caries, sinews mouldering and bodily decomposition as a whole, mortifying in ricocheting cascades. I progressed, and encountered a translucent cage, wrought of glass, I could discern nought of repugnance, or overt decay when first glancing. Then, in the corner of that dimmed room, with a pendulous sulphur lighting its minute structure, I saw it… I saw that thing…a thing. Eyes glistening so bright, alas its smile dejecting so dark. Its soul was intact, but its dignity had been sapped in one delightfully painful gust of lassitude.

The odious wretch. This creature had somehow—do not ask me the specifics—been miscreated into a fibrous wall. Immobilised, rendered impotent. His, or its be apter, facial lineaments were torpefied, and spurned to die, as if a polychromatic flower etiolated in crepuscule. The Duke had amalgamated man and concrete—man and his foundation. It is said in the Bible we were willed from clay. I suppose this statement has now been confirmed. God has always stuck to his unfaltering words.

It dawned upon me, this fellow was D-503, his sloth had been vanquished, and quite literally, he had been given the renaissance premise of nevermore being able to move a limb. I could not bear to survey this prisoner with voyeurism, I needed to continue on. I left with a wailful tearlet coursing down my cheek.

With each blink, you could see that twinkle - that human glitter in one's eye - dissipated sans a trace. I gathered my wants to slit open my throat, one solid disseverment, and all my bales would weep out. I denied this craving, for I was not a quitter, and I shall not be shaving my cells to their endmost.

I walked to the sequent glass imprisonments, and with each cabinet, it seemed to demoralise the more Each Hadean lair was maltreated with what seemed to be the Duke's darkest depths of depravity. A woman had her bosoms mastectomized, to, in turn, be placed atop her eyelids, she was lamenting the futile while. Never mind that, as worst still, since her legs had been disjoined, the nutcracker had paid his grievous respects. The replacement for her unbosoming was to substitute it with pliant kneecaps.

The butcher of the baker's field had dissected his weakly swine. Do not get me started on what they had done to her little kitty below. If sexual manipulation ever had a face, this was the poster boy for its "me, too" paragon. My cranium had commenced inflaming, in concurrence, it appalled me in rouge disfeaturement. I had lost control of my sane temple. Flashing luridities were infecting my breath, each soiled second which I spent in this closet, the more disgusted I felt. The queer sentiments were my compulsion, which galvanised me to an inert stupor. I gazed and gloated over her, with a wenching venereal famine.

The worst part of this woman's melancholic demise was that she was alive. The hunter had not yet bestowed mercy upon his prey, he had but marked it for Death. Even the most desensitised of New York hustling narcotics could not withstand the sight of this harrowed soul. No meth, nor laudanum in the world could purge thee of such a mighty fright. I knew I had more disturbing matters to attend to, thus, I took my pride elsewhere, by giving it an adequate stride.

In the Unholy Trinity, the third instance has always caused me the greatest horror. Malice nested at the next animal farm. In awe, well, our jaw will scab, it will solidify into bedrock and intimate that you have hit rock bottom. A child, an infant, a newborn sat in sombrous despair, soothed with a pretence, syphoning at his claws. A motherless youth—that is the truth. His hands sullied, and were supplanted for his feet, with his mouth sewn shut.

A scream would have occasioned recoil, and engulfed back down the depths of his Sahara deserts. A drop of water was his ironic version of the "Hope Diamond". Dracula, Dracula, remove your tarantula from this youth's bemuse. He had the mark of the devil across his forehead: the Duke's madcap bruskwork. He ran up to the glass upon seeing me. The lost boy banged, hammered, and cracked at the impenetrable shield estranging us. The wall of China would never let any non-communists exit alive. I ruined aground, and wept for his affliction.

I perceived that he tried to weep also, however, as mentioned, with his eyelids had been sown, as if from Coraline, they were dispossessed of emitting such audible anguish. Some sudden spark of rebellion must have burst within him, as he renewed the behest of morphing into a battering ram. In inefficacy, the computer's anti-viral malware stood steady. Yet the Duke's alarms were sounded. A piercing chime rang; I arose from my mournful torpor, lest they catch me in the prying nude. The sound was all too much for me. I crawled along another throe which I had not yet remarked, lubberly scaving the glass floor at my feet.

My ignorance, mixed with the peccable trials toward his people, infuriated me senseless, but I was unaware of what dwelt behind the glass flooring. Another perplexity I had disregarded: down below, perpetuated mutants in thrall, herds of detestable sheep thronged into their diminutive Hell. I swear on the good shepherd, around twenty thousand refugees must have been deported to the Isle of Death. I took my final, unscrupulous suspiration in that errant cemetery, and erected from my praying knees, to then dart for dear life. The road runner never looked back; the maze blinds its Theseus with fear.

By divine hazard, I escaped the wrathful impudence of if they had apprehended me. I am now boxed in my cell again, and the ennui of reality, the feverous delirium, and the vile psychosis disconcerts me. I can never be normal. What is normal? Is it normal to be a societal norm, a walking Norman Bates? I suppose, perhaps, I was never true to conventions. Never an average joe.

I am too afraid to use the telephone. What if they overhear my anxiety? But they must doubtless know who trespassed?

I am too afraid to put on a light, ergo, I scruple over my untoward discoveries amidst a gloaming sea - what if they barge in, and witness me writing my letter of resignation to you?

I am so afraid I am bereaved of control. O' god, this job has taken its toll.

I am wilting in suffocation, in my own words, I can no longer shuffle the tarot cards, for they had been long foredoomed. I was handed the glum fool. I am unable to assuage my frets.

I can hear the saints footslogging in my offing. They shall burst that feeble door down any minute now. Goodbye friends, and foe, I seem to be in a purgatorial suspense. I know not who was worse, you, the U.S. government, or this portentous autocracy. Both of you show signs of megalomania. I suppose the jest is on me. I, the servient maiden, shall now submit to my ghostly fiancée, whose father, Death, is walking her down the aisle, thereupon, I shall be sepulchred with one mortal kiss - it shan't go amiss!

Scarce is understood of what befall David hereafter. Some rumour he met a goliath's excruciating decimation. Some reputed his delusions led him to the conclusion that he must start afresh, therefore, subscribing to the pale, slender Duke's red-right hand. All that is known for surety is that they threw him a grand celebration in America. His efforts were not devoid of reverence. The truth had been uncloaked, and their government had been croaked. Nevertheless, they decided it was best to give this all a rest, and let Germany's sins be absolved. After all, the frustrating puzzle had been solved, so why confound things by begriming a Tenth World War? The ninth had already petrified the West enough. Alors, Germany was pardoned, and they pursued their scientific innovations in fantasy.

And maleficence fared upon Earth, as it always does.

The Dance of the Suicidal Faun

Since the dawn when I was born, I swore I was a failure. My welkin has always been a dazzling blue, which alienated me from a pubescent age, meddling with sociable intercourses. I was at tenacious dismay, when amongst humans which in turn farther estranged myself adrift. I never quite succumbed to the confidence that others seemed to have such a superabundance of. As an infant, I recall, the melancholy would drift in waves of slow yet rhythmic mutilation. It mattered not the location, nor the situation. The pre-onset type three adolescence mopery was ineluctable. Perchance, it was given through my father's bloodwork, by dint of his agnation begifting me his own strange malady. A cruel damnation. Nevertheless, I still took part in the fatal game of chess, and husbanded my dolour through the cheerless labyrinth of we whom all suspire. The pawns were in place, always leaving a rather dubious trace.

I can recollect when I thought it brilliant to displace my queen. I had the utmost faith in her, however, she was smitten down, time and time anew. The chime and chime of an unruly beast made a feast out of my failure. I grew up fast, in a Mercedes car pumped with the adrenal glands of a tiger, prepared to launch its claws profound into its wailful prey.

Nay, though I grew up fast, I did not make quips about the ability to let bygones be bygones. Erelong this led to the chalice of wine condescending, and Notre Dame's dame bursting. An entangling thallus fecundating its yokes in my previous negligences. Now I reside with no bride; just excruciation, alcohol, and I - lest we forget about my pack of smokes, from which I incessantly take tokes. Every night, I sang with ecstasy to my refuse full of gin, "You and I, we behove together like throes to woes, we are forthwith with remand."

Your response to this may be to shun what I have declared, you may have started awestruck, and ended starstruck. I implore, though, that you bless my ignorant soul, for not all hearts are suffused with coal. The lifeful glove doesn't fit all sizes. And well, if the glove doesn't fit, you must acquit.

My liver woke to exploitation. I would give her a quiver and a shiver; I was aiming for liver cancer on a silver platter. Jaundicing my entrails with a guttural roar of self-barbarity. The lungs headed full throttle for emphysema, as I inbreathed bootless clouds of clag. Any newborns were certain to inherit leukaemia. Blood transfused with whiskey, carmine wine as of a Grecian hest, and beer—the sheer amount of liquor being consumed was enough to put down an army of Spartans. Cartons rife with meads of tobacco plantations, migraines profuse with ethanol, and buckets of deterioration with no commiseration. The last checkup with a man of medicinal practices resulted in me being hurled into contumely. He cried that I was due for oedema, my Colima was due to blow at any extemporaneous moment. I left with a diagnosis of a rare affliction of my internal organs having arteries clogged to the brim with doles. Did any of the aforesaid deter me, or spur me into a life of celibate retribution? Nay, my pharos was too bleared to redress my bedraggled purity.

We do not choose to be born into sentience. We are but betrothed to exist, sans consent, and made to walk the aisle until its end. What if one rebukes the paradox of being alive, since, for them, it has spoiled to ugly tedium. Is there a purpose for bidding through lonely languor? When the wedlock between you and gaiety are effaced. Couching in an awful bridewell of unquiet shame? The whilom peaceable clock no longer chimes, but maligns. Dejected to the extent of disowning oneself of life is beyond the cogent marges of societal customs, though commoner than presupposed, nowadays. Can the acute serration of a katana be justified? These untoward meditations trampled upon my firmity, as if an insomniac.

It was a violent night—a silent kind of night. A night when the gremlins lurk, the faun's smirk, the banshees are in a fit of berserk rage, and the hydra hisses and dismisses, in defiance of their parents ordains. It was the commercial holiday every advertisement company adores, the most wonderfully fabricated time of the year. Let us say it with plenteous mirth: 'twas the night before Christmas. I lacked an Eve to spend this jolly eve with, all that was left for me to do was grieve. I had thoughts of rolling up my sleeve to slice and dice my nerval train tracks.

Depression is an immense compression of the sentiment one feels, if they have such an ennui. It cannot be rendered down, and language cannot be simplified into some 1984 novella, if one seeks to fathom it. One cannot be at ease with such a disease, depression wishes not to appease. Reasons to be cheerful, and seasons be tearful for a man who is always fearful. When you tell someone of your condition, it is often met with prejudice, they chant:

"Sad man, there's no need to feel down,
I SAID, SAD MAN, take your pill!
It will rid you of your frown
Sad man, why can't you be a clown!
I SAID, SAD MAN, take your antidepressant
SAD MAN, what do you wanna be?
Do you wanna be unpleasant, you peasant!
There are pills you can take:

Cipramil, Priligy, Prozac - lest we exterminate good olde Faverin.

They can romanticise your dystopia to a novel utopia!

So do us a favour, and take y'a pill. "You're giving us the chills."

How about nay? It is nobody's business but my own, therefore, I shall politely decline.

Do you mind if I choose to desist? Get my gist? Please don't be pissed. It is not personal; it is but business.

I thought that all my body needed was sex, drugs, and rock and roll—my frivolous ways. The wisdom of intoxicant haze. I was a malicious blockhead; I was as baseborn as love's lorn. Daffy Duck was now prepared to fire his Glock until defunct. Boys keep swinging, and men keep swigging. I poured myself a rather gluttonous serving of gin, and backed her down my oesophagus, acidizing it with a hoarse reverie. I immolate myself, with one terminal inhalation of a tortuous cigarette.

Adorning my vapid room, with the seductive tint of tarry mystique.

I now had a razzle in my pocket, primed to dazzle my mind—my own twisted witch doctor. Some ponderous medicinal cure, nonetheless, I was adamantine. I hefted her up, from my taut jeans to slay my sordid genes. Alas, as her glittering figure rose to my eyeline, all I could hear were plangent whimpers from her cylindrical nozzle.

Michelangelo's divine sculpture spoke to me with an outcry of dissension. She coveted not to be the proprietor of such ultra violence. Her gelid mussels nestled bare within the crevices of my ear canals. Her cock was cocked and loaded, ready to ejaculate all over its whore rueing for a requiem. O' lord, absolve her of her sins, she meaneth not to begot death, it is her maker who gifted her with this purpose. A wandering Staffy, and the mercenary owner bred her with monetary vexation in mind. Her cursor stuck in contemplation of wherefore she must inflict enmity, and abet prejudices.

The birth of a nation, the reincarnation of D.W. Griffith, a sniffling overture. O' William, do tell me why I am a crustacean bereaved of its carapace. Why must I dwell, with my anguish swelling, and no incubus to assuage within? Give me the strength to, at least, put my pitiful pathos in a pit of impermeable gloom. Her silencer barked through the walls of my satellite dishes. She pleaded, she needed me to surrender this ambitious endeavour. Gun shells in the gun store shoot sharp, spiteful expunction at their victims. I was to be one of these victims. My finger toyed with the curved hook, and my hand shook, quacking with lecherous apprehension. Its brittle handle made no peace of my unease.

I wish I could have been a gladiator. No, I retract that statement. I wish I could have been a samurai, and have dignity in what I was committing. Yet there was no dignity, nothing but malignity. There it was, just like a Fleming novel, and my quantum of solitude was to be impromptu embosomed at a halt. My moment of solace was to betide. Before I wielded the valance to stupefy amort, a knock came from the door of my butchery. I contemplated for an ardent five seconds whether to ignore the beckoning, and continue what I had started by ending it all, or to be courteous by unfastening the door, and admitting my pending guest; I opted for the latter.

I unhooked the latch, as, in swift, I downed another morsel of gin. Plummeting down the prodigal hatch. Widening the egress, a draught cooled by my neck, and melded around it to then engird my nape. I trembled through a delightsome bafflement. With my crystal keel of liquor held in my left hand, and carcinogenic death stick to my right, my visitor inspected me up and down. I must have appeared to be a tramp, a holiday brochure for a narcotist from Philadelphia. The man before me did not bore me, on the contrary, he riveted my anxious nerves. His face was masked by the opacity of the darksome eve, and his bowler hat added more obscurity to his recondite nature. All I could make out in the caliginous night was the white of his cornea, his irises were not brown, blue, or even the most sought-after forest green.

They were some Mary Shelley fabrication, some Frankenstein monstrosity of white. They were racially motivated. A Caucasian cornea. This curio pretended to the transparency of his appearance, with his attire being of a woollen suit, and oxford shoes. The contrast between his attire and my dire pyjamas, reeking as if miscellaneous spirits and a steam train had been inbred. Tobacco Bourbon by Tom Ford—not that I could afford such extortionate prices. He raised his hand as a signal, "Well, are you going to be neighbourly enough to usher me in?" I nodded with mumchance, and manoeuvred my lumbersome weight across to a vacancy, so as to permit his entry into my castle.

He spoke no words as he ingressed, he was as silent as a reverberant crematorium. The dead themselves susurrated through the veil of this congenial wraith. As still as your grandmother's grave, and yet, his stillness bawled a thousand politesses. We slid into my office, where I had been residing prior to his knock on my wood. Who would've known a speechless spectre, a slender, tender man, would knock but instants I forfeited my bell bottom blues. I articulated an undisguised manner, and questioned whether he would appreciate a cup of tea, or merely needed a good old-fashioned wee. The ghostly visage stared at the revolver on my desk.

"Did I-I interrupt…anything important?" said the nameless, with serene tranquillity.

Though his words were filled with the utmost sincerity, he knew the act of martyrdom that was laid ere both of our appetites. Therefore, as any good atheist would, I saw this opportunity to hide the verities of the matter.

"No, no, you did not, I was just getting some work done," I sought to further ossify my specious comment, "It has been dreadfully busy, with the odious festivities, and such." Beaming an irrespective malcontent.

The man nodded, and once more, his mouth was sewn shut, as if swathed by a ventriloquist. The Yggdrasil tree faced deforestation afresh. The uncanny visitor pranced around my untenanted room. It was as though a man of the sententious law was investigating me for a cloddish homicide —the trial of the innocent melancholiac.

The presidential candidate grasped a cherished photograph of my quondam child, lifting it to his glass marbles. The weeping angel showed signs of sorrowful remorse, his coarse eyelashes frowned with commiseration. My counsellor was swimming in my shallow pool of existence, gasping for some intel about what infatuated me. The austere sleuth, by an arbitrary miracle, called my name, and ushered me over.

"Please sir, could you make me an Irish coffee," twirling my maudlin child, "and then we can intercourse over the matter at hand." His pronunciation was magniloquent and sedative.

I did plumb as instructed by fabricating him a scolding hot Irish coffee, certifying that I use my finest aged whiskey from Dublin, pigmented like an autumnal octogenarian. I had been savouring it for a leaden and inclement day, and, though not even a tinted cloud lurked outside my moonlit drive, I made an exception for such an exceptional guest. If this is a test of my earnest soul, thought I, then so be it. Tonight, I was to be a sociable zealot, a duteous faun whose heart is to be torn. We acceded on sitting aloft some seats, after a cumbersome intermission of both our erratic personalities clashing (well, more so, on my part), abrading against one another in brutality. He loafed and purloined me of my most beloved chair. It was of Japanese heritage, with a turquoise ceramic aurora to it: depicting a wyrm who erected and flagellated a hangman for his abhorrence. It may have been my abode, yet I had been dealt the three of clubs, and was deserted upon a frigid and hard mahogany stool with no backrest. I felt as though one fatal mislean, and I would fall into the creeks of Helheim.

At last, my partner formalised our marriage proceedings, and I was given some lucidity as to why I had been so impudently aborted. The man never took his hollow spectacles off me. Each word seemed to combust a scientific reaction within him, as each syllable provoked an evermore perceptible reaction within myself.

"Look, my boy, I know, you know, and everyone knows what act of indecency you were about to commit. Your sinful want for termination, your egocentric seeking of spiritual awakening. My boy, to forsake asinine couth - I have always loathed etiquette - call me Lazarus. I, too, was once in your chap-fallen armour. I, too, once saw no light, but a mere inkwell of black stars circling a minatory nullity. When life has smarted and sieved all possibilities for your mind's ability to see clarity, do not grab your gladius.

"Do not be a bull of a man and take to crude dalliance. Nurture your vitality, get upon one knee, and you will see she shall want to be affianced. Today, much like a carol I am certain you have read tenfold, I will example the malices of your forfeiture. I hope to display the trail of the virtuous assailant to set you assail on the right rail, the correct divagation. To force you again back into the civilised mainland. Sophisticate you aboard the marine to the Isle of Man."

Lazarus uttered nonsensical rhymes, what he spoke of lacked coherence and direction. I needed him to mutter it in plain, I wished not to be deceived by some conceited cunt - as was wont in my dismal life. I was arrantly conceived with a perfervid incuriosity. I was a wild child, a Jim Morrison with a tab of lusciously soiled psychedelics. Angels' breath and Devil's dust. I, now a suicidal faun cosseted by pique, knew not that my nose bloomed as stalwart as a keratin on a rhino's horn, a brewing stew of sworn secrecy betwixt the thorny bush. I had been savouring a temptress by the name of Mary Jane for an unscheduled moment, and well, the moment had come. I uncloaked her from the clandestine, and blew on my weedy drum whilst my partner explicated the Pythagorean theorem:

"Dissimilar to my predecessor, I will elucidate your narrative in three acts myself, not with the aid of some foreign immigrant. Your past, your present and your future are all sides of this triangle. If pieced together, they form the most delectable realisation. A peculiar actualisation. Let us commence these legal proceedings, the advocate is ready, the jury is primed, and the judge is set, therefore - fire the barbette!" as he exclaimed, his irises ignited with a periwinkle crepuscule.

This penultimate sentence morphed our surroundings into a cinematic 3D experience. A puerile novelty that had been gentrified to a substandard quality. We began first with the reliquaries of my hymeneal forepassed. Before us, was I. I stood by my wife, both hands interlocked, and the hieratic locksmith had declared we may now embrace. What ensued was a damp web of kisses, tonguing aswoon our solemnised love. Two serpents swayed in unison; it brought a tear to my golden globes. I had long since eschewed her memoirs into a World War II bunker, pestilential control had disciplined the pest, and soothed my phobia to rest.

Extempore, her chalk swan dress disfeatured into sable robes, as of a Victorian relict repining for her paramour. The woman in ebon masted adroit in the fore of our peepers; we, the Toms, were guilty of monogamy. Her violet eyes, like a gorgeous wreath of asters, commenced constricting, and her blood vessels desolated from African salvation. It was the day it all ceased, the misery of when she and I departed, the morrow the tower of Pisa ruined aground, the tragedy of when Pompei said nay to its artless populace. The dominos tumbled, and our argument over my inner-repressed antipathy spited my vices in action. Fay's dictions were full of conviction, yet rightfully so. Her marbles now had a scarlet appearance, and sans a blink she verbalised the hurt in her eyes. I had, since our introductory whetting, despised that inexpressive gawk. In the wind, a throng of multifarious insects winnowed, as of a verminous haboob. They were banqueting off my sinister memoir.

"Our love was meant to last, however, you cast me to Belfast. Our once-heavenly broadcast now makes viewers aghast with gothic chloroplast."

As the ultimate riddle left her flood barriers, she vanished. David Blaine's magic had evoked in me a great bane. Despite this pitiable Lucia ceremony, it only brought forth more Norse keens. Icelandic waves of fear surged my eyes. I knew what was to succeed. The consecutive conjuration was to be my misprised child, Saul, whose life had been but a misadventurous choir of lonesome harps. A disconsolate demonstration of scurvy. Lazarus supped at his Ireland of hot drollery, and disheartened me the more; for voila, we presaged, thither idled my beauteous boy, little Timmy. It harkened in me the sentiments of how his lustre had glistered

O' so brightly. The day he spawned into this indurate world, I recall feeling as puissant as Zeus, since my boy had empowered me with some masculine affinity for infinite bliss.

The joyous proceedings shifted, when he somehow crawled out of a window. I was domiciled on the thirteenth floor, ergo, when his head impacted with the concrete, it had instigated such lurid force, that his cranium excreted its sanguine onto the pavement. Weeping the guileless ichor of a virtuoso. He was supposed to have left me that night, he was supposed to be at his mother's, - my ex-wife's mansion. My selfish longings had lured him into the divine temptation of staying another tiresome eve. It was not right. I had been the perverted perpetrator. Lazarus, with some mystical wand, paused the fabulous reincarnation at hand, and let me respire some innocuous air. Recuperate from the heinous viscera pertaining to my faults. If I had but been shrewd and diligent with him, he would never have acquired the chance to saunter along a grisly vertigo.

"You see, this is your miserable past, a wearisome evocation of atrocity trailed you. Though you may tire of viewing these terramorphous horrors, this is your irrefutable, and immedicable reality. We know what sequence followed this calamity: you spiralled, your compunction plummeted under leagues unfathomable. To quell the inquietude, you entreated the cherubs for a nepenthe, and thus, confided in the purport of chasing Kim Novak into Hades, deigning to supreme inebriation, and changed into a condemnable chimney sweeper. Now, my boy, we shall traverse into the present - behold!" His waggish eccentricity raptured me into absolute submission. When faced with terror and folkloric caprice, there is gout which sweetens the aversion presumed to be a donnée.

With these words, the blindfold had been unravelled. I, the prisoner under captivity, was finally paroled. Disparate to hitherto, where we were but perplexed by some visible screening of my past, the present differed. The room we were situated in beforehand dematerialised, under some helm of intangibility. Everything gravitating around us was void; we were maundering through some adventitious universe: the bleak canvas of a mad artist. Before our comprehension, in what seemed as though aeons away from Earth, was a man. In your ordinary and typical painting accoutrements, he looked like the finest squire. His brush had no honed and crinite nib to it, there was no whimsical brush to bespatter with, it was but a wooden stick. I could hearken the velveteen violin of Freddie's mercurial voice, willing me to acquiesce to the bestiality of life. Where Freddie was issuing from, I could not deduce, although I minded not.

Nevertheless, the fine squire's distraught neck, in a circular motion, turned to confront us, and he gave a gallant genuflection, thereupon commencing his masterly wonders.

His rhythmic movements entranced us both; my visitor paralleled my credulity, for he was as unsuspecting as I was of these unearthly circumstances. He transpired as the mere gateway to these happenings, not the actual orchestrator behind its magic. In an Edvard Munch style of rigid brushstrokes, he assailed his unending canvas - the world was his salty oyster! An ocean pervaded of brine, for him to unleash his envisagement's darkest opine. Up, down, horizontal, vertical, landscape, and portrait the movement did not cease. The marathon was to be won with ease. Meanwhile, he perspired and emulated a crude bayou, pouring his entire quintessence into this machination.

Even the world's most skilful athletes were no match, this Michael Phelps was a supernal deity. It all discontinued at an abrupt celerity; a learner driver had failed to comprehend the prerequisite for shifting gears, therefore, the car came fiercely to a perilous impediment. Images of me confounded me, and roiled in a faint. One portrayed diverse bottles of poison encircling around me, each whispering amoral lullabies. Another, fancied me being enshrouded in an Oriental carpet, held in an unmalleable grip which was engendered by myself; then a kindle was lit, and I fired ablaze. It seemed I was inclined to smoke my animate exoskeleton, notwithstanding it jeopardising me deathwards. Not even the most august samurai would be braced for such macabre certitude. The last depiction was of all my previous acquaintances, whom I had long pretermitted. They were disconcerted, and knocked upon the derelict door of my barren abode. I resolved that I wished not to accommodate even my most trusty subjects. Their faces were inflamed with pensive heartbreak. They yearned for a capitulation. Where was I? Why was I so egregious? Did I find this tragicomical play humorous? This artist had welcomed a sense of solidarity amongst my fellow men in arms. It was a feeling I could no longer negate, nor inearth under the soil of my recurrent vicissitudes. A game of disregardful seeking for some furtive simpleton.

Nay, I could not remove this yearning, my unrest fluttered sternly upright. I cannot hide the fact that I was mystified by his preposterous masterdom.

Then, with a blow of his alveoli, the hurtful images sailed off to some foreign Galactica, and once more, he set to work.

In this instance, it embodied a repugnant edge. I saw eight-legged creatures to whom bore my head as theirs, I witnessed sallow daemons cleaving the flesh and organs from my very own cadaver. Most horrifying of all was a cyclops, who, with his singular monocle, gazed upon my soporous body. Polyphemus the letch gaped, with grotesque eroticism, into an integral part of my pith.

His grimace quivered with erection. It was as if Sir Allan Poe and Odilon had both belaboured to doctor to animalise a brutish gyrification. I had not been intrepid enough for these sights. I bellowed a cry of exasperation, a protest so loud, the government would have to listen for once. The present exited, and we were transported back into a familiar realm anew.

"Apologies, my boy, I know that was infernal, awful, and even satanic, however, it was essential. Now, I forewarn you, the future will not appeal to you, either. The sooth is often scornful.

I am not a phantast but we dwell not in fantasy. This is your reality, as humans know it, with the whim of your woes skulking."

With these words, we began my final hearing amongst the court of anomalies. The cassette oscillated, and played my linear anecdotes again. It was I, denuded upon the floor, flaunting my arse, my vermillion guts strewn, and fraught with my cranium's pulpy corporeality. Stranger still, pieces of the sinuous jigsaw could be seen in the fish tank I had long forgotten; at least they had some nourishment, considering I never fed, nor cared for them - the lambs could silence their protest. Yes, it was disgusting, nonetheless, it occasioned little to no melancholy within me.

A knife was impromptu transpierced through my heart and spleen. A vicious painting lay before me, wisped by a churlish Neanderthal. It was my glorious mother; she reposed beside me, her eye sockets effervesced, collapsing with decompression sickness, and from her mouth erupted volcanic bile. The delineation was vile. My sister was next to join the queue of rue. Of course, she strode in condescension, albeit upon seeing my unconscious state and disfigurement, ferocious goosebumps proliferated. My sister could not maintain that venturous courage of hers, which she was so renowned for. Courage the cowardly dog, denigrating in dogging her sorrow aloud. In fine, was my ex-lover, my ex-partner, on whom keening resounded from my amatory and hateful crime.

My once best friend. Her pupils thawed with large froths of fear, impregnated by despondence. It was clear she was overwrought and distraught. Her mind coarsened with ligneous conjunctivitis. It bled from her pores. Here were three broken souls, three chasmic holes ailing in their psyches. They all arose in behindhand from the dead, la folie commence en nuance. Mes gens d'armes sont tous fous. The gunmen wrenched their pump shotguns, and americanised their hecatombs with all vehement guns. It was polarising. This Christmas carol no longer was joyously sweet, the carolling had taken a reverse for the worse.

The malison had begun adulterating. The display of dolour was meriting a medal of valour to any who suffered its hideosity. All those times my conscience had spent quarrelling with itself, for it to lead to me being fordone, in turn, causing such a horrid sequel. The Big Bang had been, with gaucherie, shown on some power point presentation by some degenerate wolf of Wall Street. The smart was not over, for the princes, the queens, and the Augustan praetorians marched in. The saints of my just acquaintances rolled in, and seeing their cherished ones suicide the same fate as myself, decided it was only lawful to retrieve their AK 47's, and set voyage for the netherworld. My ciliary muscles narrowed to near extinction with the conviction I witnessed.

Ah, the bitter glory of love, the integrity of companionship. It always wildered me how, for olde folks who have been engaged in wedlock for myriads of winters, when their partner perishes, they cease to exist also. It is too tempting to resist the euphony of disharmonising alongside them. In truth, my baleful errors of yesteryear had been one to transcribe into the books.

The show abruptly ended. My partner once more glared inside me.

The show may have ended, nevertheless, he knew what I had observed would forever live on within. This was to be my novel sin, which I must pass on to everyone's kin. He spoke his concluding concoction.

"Though you may not admit to the grit you have undergone, deep inside lurks a reformation. Doth behove new honour and new self-worth. I ought to quit now, knowing your scruples have been deterged. You have been sanctified and rectified, your soul be protestantical. If you do proceed with your frolic with melancholia, be certain I shall see to it that you cremate in hell. Your turtle shell is certain to reckon with scorching burdens, your corpse will become the human torch. I will vindicate you to be cauterised. Farewell, and I blest you hath good morrows to come! "

With these words, his lanky silhouette pearled, and then disappeared amidst the wan moonlight. The time was apt, I felt fit to start from rudimentary scratch. I felt it was right to be a fool, and purchase some inane scratch card - foreknowing of its futility - to place my bets upon how long my sobriety would last. Nay, these were negative ambitions, I persuaded myself otherwise, and quashed all of the vices I could find. That night (to be frank it was almost dawn, by the hour I had reached my pile of fainéant hay) I slumbered like no infant has ever. Never had I ever dreamt of such tranquil serendipity. Persuasion, Pride, and Prejudices are all illusions from henceforth. I was reborn, my figure prostrated upon the lavish cross, though no vexation could be smelt through my fortitude.

What eloped, through the scenes of these absurd occurrences, bemuses me still. It was something alluding to a reverist's carnival. Lazarus had enveloped my core by sourcing to then purge me of my ills, misgivings, and guilt, which I had sepulchred and forbidden from the hue of morn's sun. I seldom dwell on the confusion, since, in the main, inexplicability is best left unresolved. All the same, I shall forevermore be in arrears to Lazarus.

We click fast-forward, and here I am, still alive and kicking, simple-minded as ever, yet jungle land has never been so regaling. Merriment appears sans much travail; hysteria harrows itself through the revoking of self-pity. Now listen here folks, who would've thought I, a man who faced many drunk and disorderly charges, could transfigure to be as clean as a freshly douched arse crack? Do not misconstrue: I am no cupid, but trust me when I say I am nevermore stoned, nor stupid. I want to walk, not be carried, I want to remain married... Married to my heavenly sobriety of happiness. I encounter saddening billows, however, I repulse them afar off, and deal with them in a prudent tact.

Society may judge you for your views, even vitiate you for having depression. They want you to be their muse and amuse their every piety. Who has got news for Hughes? We do, their impiety has gone on too long, they can sustain their state of inebriety, by remaining abstinent. A deadly inhalant for one with decompartmentalization, human nature is like a divalent atom, the Jekyll and Hyde, you can hide your misery with vice, yet it always catches up twice as fast. The jaguar is an impassioned predator.

I suppose you may say, damn you are a new gentleman! - well, hold the bridle on your presumptuous horse, for nay, though I am on par with an aspiring route, I am taking the M25 up to a fortunate son of mine. The quarry is where I lay my worry. My welkin is still blue, although I grieve past its blinding dazzle. I am as dry as a seven-year drought, and with little doubt, I shall strive to arrive at some form of cloud nine - it will be mine. I wish to make amends, connect with lost friends, and this is where my story ends.

The Changeling

Everyone has heard the ghoulish tale of Mary and her bloody ways, everyone has heard the rumours of the ironic tale of the apian Candyman, for he afflicts pain, not sweet treats.

Everyone knows of the infamous Jack and his ability to rent through bawdy ranks of London's prostitutes. We all know of Henry and his six wives; some whereof ended up being headless. Napoleon and his transfixation on world dominium, his efforts to indurate Europe into one nation. Jeepers, creepers, son where did you get all this knowledge? A true magician never reveals his privies, that would render him seedless and needless. Here is one tale I am certain none of you arrogant fools have yet come across, in your hollow and bright lives. Allow me to broaden your minds to the amity I am to bestow upon you all. I am often cited as an undependable narrator.

It is said, with a great deal of dread, that a man is given three chances. A cat is given nine, but nein, we are unworthy of such boons; we would manipulate, or abuse such benefaction. We - men and women alike, therefore, have three strikes, and we are deceased. It matters not if he or she shouts from the rooftops of Odin's palace, nor if he drinks from Zeus' chalice - 'tis three strikes, with no possibility of quarrelling otherwise, as of incompatible doves. Now you may ask, what happens if one flouts these strict confines? Well, it is foretold, in italics, that the Changeling will forge it as his callous contest to expedite you as his sequent conquest. You cannot run from the hunt, nor can you hide, for your hands become tied. The Gordian knot knits its ovules, and impregnates you with despair.

With the introductory formalities out of the way, let us make way for our protagonist. At the start, I had resolved upon elucidating his Christian name, however, I found him too vulgar to deserve such sympathy, therefore let us traduce him as the Chiseller. Picture this innominate painting which I shall daub in your fores. This man was far from conversable, far from benignant, and far from genteel. He awoke to a bowl of human tears. He gratified off on seeing people's towers come crashing down in full force. He only had eyes for your deepest despondency; he was reliant on this. As a child, he grew up in a rough neighbourhood, and his means for affording the yeast, for his comestible breed, was to pickpocket, purloin, and pillage communal establishments.

This profession is suitable for someone of but juvenile and slender tenor, which meant, once he had matured and attained the height of 5.7, at age of sixteen, he handed in his slip of resignation and researched for occupational applications. With no education in his portfolio, this endeavour was forlorn. What do you do when your resume is blank, unclear, and insincere? Crime, conniving, and farcical veneers. He, instead, gloomed his etch identity through the chicane of solemn integrity. As the years progressed, he juggled in selling black tar and hoary gold, though he found it too onerous in its impracticability, and dissolved from being a paragon of the narcotic industry. He must be responsible for innumerable deaths, since many regarded his toxins as pure, pious even to his fast competitors, when all the while he was wringing them of their monetary milk, and enfeebled them with lethal horizons.

Nevertheless, that petite slice of crime aroused the Chiseller: he enjoyed seeing these lifeless, skeletal figures plead and supplicate by prostrating upon their importunate knees in some debauchery of nuptial proposal, for one last three-five on loan, in spite of their exquisite arrears. He knew the area of expertise he was to tease in. He put all his bread into one chicken, one quaint abode, which he renovated into some sort of penny stock trading centre, where he wrought to incapacitate credulous fawners. He christened his novel talent with the title of "The Grimsby Jewelly". He had expected this to be another otiose venture, alas, it prevailed, his shop assailed its customers, his clientele failed to be informed of the illegitimacy of the enterprise, and the fraudulence swindled them of their toilsome wherewithal.

The homely town, time and time again, with their beloved philtres, assayed fiercely to burn the reputation of the Chiseller aground. Yet it is harder than conceivable to extinguish such a cunning supernova. He had been sired with insolvency, whereas now his carpet was fashioned of unalloyed cowhide, the quilt of his bed woven of sheeny silk, and his suits were tailored by Alfred Dunhill. In his sympathy, it was clear this theftuous swine was of devilish origin, although people in continuum deluged his services, asking for him to "invest" their pecuniary green into some greener meads. O' how fraught with guileless trust, humans can be.

Fools sucking on their mother's thumb, vivisecting their veins open till bled dry.

Our misfortune-bestower had now stacked up quite the luscious pair of natal back ribs for himself. Wealth was all one could predict would flock to the Chiseller, genuflecting once in his immediate vicinage. Whilst he was profiting, others were perishing in baneful ways. The first suicide transpired on March 1st 1998: a female of unbeknown name placed her entire bequeathal in the mercenary hands of the Chiseller. The road runner drove his avarice, amorously, astray with her money in his wake. Upon her audit arriving, and her naive spirit panicking at the sight of no return upon her courageous gambles, she suicided her life in her basin; coral steaks freaked her lavatory, forevermore painting it with a distressful aura. She must have been douching herself amidst the pennant solace of her bath, when reality's beacon sullied, and tempted her to just take the piece of glass that, by chance, reposed on her tiled floor.

Next came a fellow by the name of Antonio. He was of necessitous descent, like our antagonist. But they differed in incomparable manners, since though this man had been defamed with the tarot card of peasantry, he had reversed such a handicap, and harvested enormous amounts of golden paper for himself. The calamity betided when one glittery but gelid morn, as he quaffed on a scalding pot of coffee to warm his senses, he read an article in the regional razzle which ran thus: "From rags to riches, from rags to bags of wealth, trust in me, and I shall provide you with boundless gold dust." For a sagacious intellectual, this offer was too wholesome to savour, alas for Antonio, it urged him to meet its maker. Antonio, ergo, at noon, telephoned this sibylline mystic and betrayed his incredible gullibility. They confessed their love over the landline, Antonio was playing with a sophist's fire by conversing with the devil. The sociable landmine which Antonio became mired within, ensued misery and trod upon his mortality. It does not take an oracle to augur the omens that occurred. The man's lifelong moils, knighting himself from pauperdom to sovereignty, diminished into miniscule atoms. He had spent so many wakeful eves, myriads of lidless lie-ins, arrays of insomnolent-festered morrows, wading through the minacity of insomnia. He chose to be a beach boy, and grasped his beretta for a personal vendetta. The intoxicating poinsettia coursed throughout, and doused his cranial flame. Another soul smote to dust.

As I forewarned, a man is permitted three chances, and this was the third to fall. A lady, by the name of Josephine, so ravishing, so rife with lavishing ardour that she could dash one's espousal. Her blue eyes were O' so resplendent, and her waxen maquillage, though she comported more than the common dame, was so beautifully blended. Her umbrous mascara shadowed the circumference of her lucid corneas and azure irises, piquing the most obstinate chastes from dormancy to erection. Now, her feet were a Tarantino fanatic's dream, O' how they curdled the pearly cream of men. One eve of sin would win her heart apart, for she was but a virginal flora. She had never confronted a hurdle in her running career - life seemed but marmalade to our feline Paddington. Her aesthetic style beguiled the attraction of nymphs, enticing men to jump from Everest. Josephine never couched in rest, for clamant gallants, and abhorrent suitors, without remission, protested their feelings of neglect. "Marry me! O' Marry me!" is all the damask rosebuds heard. She never boasted, or scolded these doltish simpletons, who threw themselves at her affectless heels. She coveted a man of irreproachable docility, not a besotted maniac.

Josephine, notwithstanding her tender rebuffs to courtships, astonished the townsfolk, and willed them to her favour. No one dared ever slander her, nor debase her with downright ignominy. Josephine had the boon of saintly beauty, to pleach everyone's esteem into her candid pockets.

She was neither wealthy, nor impoverished, yet like every other human, she wished to obtain a sturdy incline to attain opulence. The heart-broker's suasion reached her sombrous credulity, and prompted her to challenge him at a game of chess. The artful Chiseller was victorious as wont - it was an immutable surety. Alack, Josephine, the queen, the cherubic Athene—the imprecation was too formidable for her, she was no longer biddable in the game of charades. She had but no more coins left to insert into the exacting arcades.

The virginal teen underwent her surgery, she threw herself from the highest peak in the village: the vertiginous, venerable church. The village and its community could never surmount this great height, save Rumpelstiltskin. The populace bewept, per contra, upon the news reaching the abode of the Chiseller, he almost choked from chortling over this comedic tale. We may not view it as jocund, mordacious, or funny whatsoever, nonetheless, he relished in his own fictitious cozenages.

O' will nothing disembarrass us of this heaven! We pray for the sake of the townsfolk that we be endowed with an entity - surpassing the Chiseller's own disfigured miscreancy - to be awakened so as to disambiguate him of his hideous, unjust venom. Enucleate him of his visionless bale. A requiter ordained to slay the daemon through whom suicide proliferated. Mactate his head upon a pike to avouch of the Chiseller's immolation.

Some say the devil is malign, though it is hard to differentiate, since he appears in moths of differing sorts.

One day, a knock came from his iron-fastened battlement. He arose with alacrity, and unbolted his locks, yet upon peeking through a suspicious chink, he perceived no one to be present. Sheer dereliction, besides the torrid grimace of the tangerine ablaze.

In begrudgement, he distended the latch and let her respire some undefiled air, thereupon doing so, he remarked a letter sprawled on his grizzly porch. It was addressed to him in baroque fantasy, with a scriptural elegance to it. His inquisitive nature worsted the better of him, as he broke her red seal open. The injurious, vestal prostitutes were too tempting for the Chiseller's flaccid Richard. Upon reading this invitation, his finger fluttered, it flitted with forgoing fear. I will be so kind as to endorse you with the grim details. It went as follows:

"To Whom This Concerns,

You sir, shall soon curl into a fit of your own quacking pit. I have been witnessing your treachery for a century. You have had a chance with your streak of homeruns, your peepers ogling every sod you saw. Now hear me, Barry Bonds, with your merry ponds of gilt, this will now come to a cessation. You have until four am, as the sun and moon coalesce - make the most of your remaining hours, and hearken to the peals of dread.

Yours sincerely, the Changeling."

The great pretender could not help but be vanquished with sudden anguish. Who was this "Changeling", this changeful thing? did it think it could outwit a golden deity such as himself. John Connor was fueled by his obsessive-compulsive disorder to ascertain the animosity of Cyberdyne Systems. No one besmeared their gangrene-ridden hands on his red joystick, lest they could brave the repercussions. Enough is enough! He sufficed with the hauntings of a mysterious faerie - whom was he to get lairy with Larry? Wrath possessed this livid sphinx, he refused luncheon, diner, and even refused a pleasant glass of cardinal sopor.

The clock was approaching three o'clock, and the sand in the hourglass could scant stand upright. He was reading an outré novel whilst loathing over a smug pint of hot cocoa. The novel, whose arse lay wide agape in his clammy hands, was none other than a Requiem for a Dream. Incense and ice, a concerning fetor, a distinct livery hepaticus streamed merrily through his damnable household.

Moronic man, why did the pseudo-Lou opt to peruse at this present time of peril? His life was in shambles, and bushes of horned brambles launched on to his Id. The horologist of doom had arrived: the hour of unholy beings mewled. As the time delineated four am, the wilderness outside subverted from ordinary to extraordinary. In the midst of the gloaming, wondrous birds went from chirruping ballads to mutilating monodies. The pendulous moon pared his hazy opal, inverting it for the pigment of blood, as if a cruor exsanguinating. The sun, aping the lunar pallor, obeyed the forecasts of the Changeling, and was levitating in the skies, coalescing with night itself. Founts of glorious water putrefied, and verdures uglified to a vomitous colour.

The Chiseller but ceased his delightsome read, which he had always orated aloud, when these incomprehensible, obnoxious, and quizzical effects reeked throughout his once opiate halls. The harmony of a calmative zephyr was supplanted for an unquiet cacophony, which resounded throughout his domicile. They emanated from nowhere on Earth. The sole location that we can attribute these oddities to is the viscera of subterranean horrors, lying underneath our feet. They rivalled the wicked affairs of our Chiseller. A malodour swelled from his lavatory. Paranoia set in, his superego dwindled, and all that was left was rancidity. He was conflicted by two despots that spoke, and tried rationalising this irrationality. One held these circumstances in reverence, and sued him to hide, lest the secretive blight catches him. The alternate premonition fructified a false sense of keen assurance, and bid him hence to explore its origins. He had charnelled numerous bystanders in the course of his life, so why now be daunted? He validated the latter, and traipsed to the lobito, with his ego skulking as he did so. Entering the cubic nightmare, he discerned nothing awry. His mind slipped into a corroborative ease. He headed to flood his urinal with high morale, since a pang from his root canal spiked his blood sugar. He needed some insulin to root his wits in place anew. With this prideful conceit of safety, he spent a season urinating, and chuckling to himself about how fatuous his fears had been. All the while an unnerving aura was manifesting, and a vicious torrent watched him baulk the bowl. Soddening the floor with a yellowish emission.

Precluding his acidic load, the Chiseller digressed to his basin, and twisted the knob on his tap. He had twisted the frosty tap thrice, however, ominous steam clouded the lavatory. No liquid poured out. A sultry tone was being written into his narrative. All the same, he operated with nonchalance, as though the vicinity was not a helly inferno. He bore an imperious smile, projecting his glee to the apparition looming in the teething mists. His presence soon became as clear as day. The dread sank his ship, he rotated to the ineffable figure, and there stood a mythical beast. It was at this moment, that he knew he had picked from the wrong vocation in life. He wished to yell, and utter a fervid alarm, but his vocal chords were bedumbed. Even they forbade him from useless speech.

The beast stood a tremendous 7 foot tall, its claws were nigh as harrowing as his unruly roars. His pelage was embrowned by chocolate, and his tail fortified by a condescending cutlery. He had no eyes, yet one needs not the gift of vision, when clarity is your confederate. His nose must have been misguided, for it was misplaced from his face. To be trite, one needs not the gift of smell to spirit someone else's diction. The cordial (if you were an affable oaf) Changeling was something mythicised from a Kafkaesque, or Lovecraftian, piece of fiction. He was the kind of person your parents recounted to you as an infant squire, in hopes it might deter you from misdemeanours.

Our gallant made it apparent he was craven; his pigtail tied to his demise. In a streak of last-minute ambition, he repossessed linguistic capability.

"Please sir, please, you Changeling, please spare me - why care for me? I promise, if you are as lenient as to spare my soul, I shall banish those malicious intents of mine. Fine, from now on, all my omens will be magnanimous. I will renounce my forgeries, and pledge my piteous time to providing wretches with riches." No response, nor sounds, cooled out of the implacable beast.

He renewed his supplications, "I swear upon my grave I am not being deceitful!" he facsimiled his most penitent tone.

Though these words were the most unearnest lyrics he had ever sung, they did not content the Changeling, he had come for a singular reason, and no imbecile could coax him otherwise. He denied these pleas for wasteful bargaining. The parable of the fraudulent fraud was to be erased, albeit if he was to be made an example of, then the Chiseller believed he deserved a fair tribunal, and thus, deserving to know who the hangman was.

"If I am to die by your mitts, at least let my wits know who you are?" He ruined upon his knee, as he rejoined, "My veracious magistrate." toadying to the volition of his bestial visitant.

"I'm the food you eat,
The women whom you beat,
The naiveties whom you mulct,
The virtues whom you so facilely reaped atop deceit,
The waste you excrete,
I am the king who requites,

The man whose heart has been impaled, with a wooden stake.

I am vampiric revenge,

And my show is spectacular. Allow me to demonstrate."

Realisation deigned in, as the Chiseler deciphered his next station to be damnation. He had plagued this Thracian nation, and lactated it for all it was worth. Many had undergone extreme alienation, and he was the sole causation for so.

At last, his cremation was roiled in stone, and Arthur would be forced to withdraw his claim to fame. The Changeling was transporting him to the high school ball for a bloody good brawl. The Chiseller knew not what true hurt, as he had so sickened upon innocence, felt like. Paltry Chiseller had been so ignorant to those who had been obliterated by his acquisitive lighting. The reaper was to sow what he measured in arrears - he was so clueless, Cinderella was O' so shoeless. The vindictive organism, with its right claw, enucleated his left eye, and with his left claw, his right eye. His sabretooth teeth sundered his tongue from his mouth, cleaving it in one fugitive biteful of fury. He exenterated his nose down to immateriality; it was now rendered futile, and inutile. The Changeling succeeded by, mirthfully, razoring both Chiseller's ears off. His compos mentis was lobotomised, and wrung in a dank abattoir, amongst other covetous swines suspending from their hooks. His ultimate hoorah was unsheathing his phallus, quiescing behind its besuited armour, and revealed its diminutive and effete appearance, like a womanly dandelion. He and his phallus proceeded to lament, however, impromptu the Changeling circumcised to then behead its residual potence. Denatured, deconstructed, and desexualised was the Chiseller. A feeble androgyny.

The poor jello must have contracted some industrial disease, the stench of pungent Swiss cheese issued through the washroom.

What did we have left? The thinker could no longer function, David no longer fought Goliath, Christ had been redeemed, and Discobolus felt discombobulated. The wanderer was now set free to roam wherever he dared. He was hexed to walk through the limbo of death, with four of the five senses absent, they had gone on maternity leave. All that remained was touch, but how fruitful is touch when one clutches to his spineless crutch for life?

The Fisherman's Catch

Once upon a time, there was a rhyme; and upon that rhyme, there was a lake which prostrated wide awake. Some say the devil, in the form of a snake, wintered due to some lustreless heartbreak. These are strange days, fantastical chimes are heard throughout, as preternatural rhymes are being mimed; these, my friends, are the signs of our contemporary times. In the ghastly moonlight which glistered an array of nacres, fishermen would say they saw monsterful figures, malefic spectres, and execrable monsters, hovering with their hands asprawl, awaiting to catch a naive farceur amidst their horrid snares.

It was ironic when the moon befell on the earthen lands, the roles reversed, and the tenebrious phantoms were the fishermen. Sailors rumoured of hearing angelic nursery rhymes, and idolatrous sounds, leading to tragic ends, as if gulled into an Amphitheatre of doom. Piffling, sniffling sea dogs would fare from distant galaxies afar off, in search of the lucrative riches that lurked beneath the pernicious water. Pigmented cerulean upon its perceptible superficies, alas, profounder down, the leagues debased to something of unutterable consternation.

Any roguish fish imaginable, would be discoverable in this insidious lake; particular species and genera anteceded the primaeval eras, and were fossilised in a gauze of immortality. It was a pastime paradise for any who sought riches, and zealots who ravished their orbs by marine-gazing at Regal Mackerels, Waspish Garfish, Disjointed Siamese Brawlers, superabundances of Tartar Sharks - some bedizened by obsidian and sapphires, whereas others were adorned with mythical polychromes, veering away from normalcy. As one can see, the creatures were of a transcendent hypnotism. Nevertheless, nothing comes gratis. This lake, notwithstanding its aquarium of spectacular antiquities, was accursed by an unnatural puissance, deriving from whence knows where! Caching evil to such a fruitful effect, that not even an X-ray could not uncover its roily torrents. Some malignant tumours are best left to float adrift the Southern Pacific rims.

Our Prince Charming was a fisherman, however, apprehended these whispers, and found them rather alluring. A sadistic fuck, a masochistic thug. Yet, I suppose, to the minority - or, percase, majority - flamboyant wealth can exceed the most hazardous perils, even if its consequences entail the possibility of a grisly death. Some merely caper in line, and rock their cadavers on time.

Our fair Belafonte was willing to do the complete Monty for a vestige of Marie's dacquoise. He travelled forty nights and forty days to reach the intended destination. His ship perched at ease aslant, undulating to the fortissimo of the circumjacent billows. The maritime neighbours below, daunted at his inexplicable valiance, and peculiar imbecility. They, nonetheless, fancied this nautical jester to be too impudent, and warranted a moralistic metaphor to reprehend him. His courage would be startled aback, and reprise its role as timorous cravenhood. After all, our Prince Charming had felt it his duty to self-impose himself upon their marvellous waters. Well, our venturesome fool would soon learn through scourges, that he had trespassed upon the wrong door: this haunted house was vehement scouse. The fiery fury hebetated at its pivotal depths, yet to summon its unreckonable seaquake, to then pounce extempore.

The bold fisherman reared his metallic phallic anchor, and drove her right into the depths of the lake. It made her quake. She let this instance slide; she would see how far this gluttonous goat would go. His cellular reticulation was thrown into the blue mirror. The ghastly moon exonerated at his audacity, and grimaced at the brother in attempts of portending. The constellations astir, also, twinkled their sham to forbid him further. These futilities were materialised, of course. His appetite had been whetted, and his chimerical surroundings gyved him in trance.

The man could have sufficed with a mere fishing rod, and yet, no, he needed operose amounts to quench his hunger. Hunger is unfathomably seeded in those who long for fortune; it vivifies their banal existence. Above the surface, as his anchor vitrified below, our fisherman gladded at his tactless deeds by gloating, and succumbed to felicity. He multiplied his loath avarice by riving a maggot upon an acute pike on his iron rod, and hurled it across the bellicose waves; they engulfed the rod and maudlin maggot. He was all the while unawares of the malevolent force amercing with anger. As he sapped the essence out of the lake, he beheld the awesome noctilucent welkin, and, needless to reiterate, the pallid lune beside them suspended in midair. A sham quietude stole by.

On the other side of this cerulean mirror, schools of innocent children were being baited into this barbed pike, as if impaled by a viscous shrike. Schools, herds, and morgues of fish swam for mere reverie into the Hotel California, and instanter became hooked. The warlike eagle was set to feast. One by one, the Mongols were transfixed. He must have attained thousands of profitable catches by now. This was nowhere near enough. His endeavours toiled for more, he would terminate his carnage but when they rife surfeited his unstable keel. With this mentality, he ascertained it would be all the more advantageous, if he were to throw another spider's web into the mix, add a skewer more Cajun spice into the recipe. He did as his greedy psyche decreed.

More innocent infants were slaughtered—more unknowing babes, in a state of arrant mania, swivelled to the treacly bait upon his pike. The slaughterhouse five at the lake's crux awakened to the damnation. Bibliomania had taken over. The black snake raked in his meat. He had transgressed too far, his errors were too potent and unpardonable, his Dior Sauvage aromatised too pungent - they cherished squire Depp, alas not to such astringent effects. He had sprayed too many sickly-sweet scents with his diffuser. It was nighing daybreak, when the cockcrow of dawn heralds it a new day to be reborn. He had abused his power for the nocturnal season, and therefore, would not be let off lightly. His vanity had gazed into the fallacious mirror. His prognosis is terminal vanity.

His glow fluttered, and the Doberman's canine senses unleashed. Betwixt a darker patch of cerulean terrain movement was present. It was beyond his feeble buoys to reach, and they thwarted to entrap it; he designed the failure as a personal vendetta against his ego, hence, a necessary task to complete. He took out his fishing wand, and set forth to decrypt the unsolvable riddle. Humbert constructed his simulation of a shop, with a leviathan sign which read "free candy", in his best enticements to lure Lolita towards his artificial angler fish's pike. As he did so, an overbearing blister of pride sagged from his cranium's breasts.

He was to be the sole survivor of this revered reservoir; he could be crowned the predatory pharaoh. Without a doubt, he would be dubbed the scornful scarecrow, baiting his victims with Cairo's lapis lazuli. His cheeks crimsoned rosaceous from such precarious presages. It was clear the man had dreams he wished to fulfil. James rejoices at tales of Ulysses, and Homer adores an Odyssey, and our prince charming elates at usurping undue exaction. He was very much into theosophy; the appraised Catherine Laveau would soon grant his wish—ahh how she once was so belle! Pardon my voyeuristic intervention, I avow that I am in the process of being rehabilitated for nymphomania. The road is a feverous nightmare to abstain from.

The sailor had hit gold, since his rod firmly clasped to some alien lifeform. He began to reel his wheel in, though he met an imponderable resistance. His frustration overwhelmed him, and his charity forfeited. Doctor Barnados smiled no more; his joy had been washed ashore. You're lost, little mademoiselle. Sphere into a formidable scoliosis, and show us your underlying fear. Show us your rear, pirthee, dear. It was so queer, he could hear nothing but the waves of Aphrodite, the German mermen slumbered. He took it upon himself to use his pike so meretriciously the thing would surrender. As a retaliation, that cerulean limpidity marred itself to an irreversible tenebrosity. He dismissed this metamorphosis, instead, he redoubled his efforts at exerting his utmost.

Ambitiously, his studs rubbed the wheel, the cord burned, and an effeminate triumph at last prevailed. His rod soothed and rose the cord from the stygian lake. His hook rose, she gasped for air, there on that fateful snare stood nothing. No splendid fish of ancient marvel, no treasure flirted with his eyes, no luscious brilliance hoisted up alongside Captain Hook. His hand shook with trepidation. His feet quivered with stupendous poltroon. His legs plied in ways one could not even ideate. With immediacy, he needed a priest to perform an exorcism, before he devolved into a Grecian statue. Prince Charming was affronted, and impinguated his umbrage by crying through the whistling wind. His patience attenuated, as his mortal tightrope slimmed aground.

With his bare fists, in ape-like wrath, he unleashed his choler. His antipathy infected the impeccant inky-blue lagoon. The lakish lagoon had tired of being told it was ruthless, when, in reality, it was but protecting its offspring. It sneered its foot down. A promiscuous wife, whose ogre of a husband incessantly sups his larger, whilst in concurrence cracks at her rear, occasioned a flood with a crystal tear. She had been beer-battered for the ultimate time; or, perhaps, penultimate be apter still. Poseidon saw his divine wife bewail for the final misadventure. Our nautical Prince had violated his last crime. Cetus unleashed its beloved foetus through uproarious ill-humour.

Our sailor reproved the progression of his simpleton cracks and whacks at an inanimate object, he wagered that the waters were causing him to hallucinate. Those ripples he had espied were but naval mirages, common amongst his kin. He now resumed his spectatorship of the heavens, as he inbreathed some tobacco from his birchen woodpipe. The spheroid tip of his pipe blazed a witching orange. The water began frothing round and round as penance went round, incarnating a Charybdis of ghouls, and cesspool of wicked sea demons. A cruel garden of carbon monoxides roiled in his fore. In the midst of this circular and clockwise pirouette, an atrocity ascended from its marine tomb. First, our sailor saw its flexuous locks, and, O' my, were they far from golden. Wires as dark as East Crimea, entangled in a mixture of seaweed and raw flesh. Her hair was as thick as an archaic knight's armour, fashioned chiefly of sooted mesh. Insuperable by human enfeeblement.

Coarse stubs of the viny hair shifted towards the sky, as the corpse bride hefted her veil upwards. Next came the eyes. Coal-black pupils dilated, and the whites of her eyes had long been castrated. The muscles in her eyes had long ceased to function, they shone beams of grievous delight, it was a couth sophisticated by spurious charlatans. The sinuate meat attiring her profile was diabolical, she had decorated herself with a helly clown's makeup, consisting of viscid leeches and variegated nudibranchs.

Slime exuded from her beefy countenance. Bubbles of pustules kept her features aghast, like little embryos of oil. The woman needed plastic surgery by the NHS to beautify her hideosity. Her vengeance inflated and simulated the movements of her spinous skeleton. Her skin had features of a Kraken's suction cups, her teeth were as serrated as that of a crocodilian Makara, her scales were as spiculose as that of a Jormungand. This play had commenced as a comedy, and was now concluding as a sinistrous tragedy. Our Marlon Brando was aboard a streetcar named despair. You seem to be in quite the mare, Claire. Her breasts, impugnable to the plasticity of her beef languished, sagged; her once hourglass rigidity was no longer apparent. She uttered a short but absolute speech.

"My eyes have seen you, our eyes saw you whilst you plundered us - you can face me and stare in fair pleas, nevertheless, this will be your last misogynistic glare."

He was precluded from disguise; his television skies were going to abscise and reprise his disguise. Her photograph captivated your soul, despite its terrifying attributes, ensorcelled you in your stead; as if being gifted coal at Christmas time, it made you discontented yet appreciative. The banshee's screech killed the rhetoric drummer, hibernating his ears. He was now deaf, and soon to be made redundant. When the music's over, the poser will be dealt in a manner that is far from kosher.

The composer lost his composure, and started to inch closer and closer. Sirens, from an invisible cavern, plained, the Jamaican wailers hollered, and an audible though inscrutable clock tolled. He was petrified and maniacal and could not relax. He was unable to face up to the facts. Réalisant son salaire, il fut effrayé par une défaite morose.

Her serpentine tail propelled her with celerity through the ocean's grievance. The princely outlander's hazard dawneth.

They were now face-to-face, the chase for some Chinese lace was already finished. The question now remained: would they take things to second base? O', they were to be more lascivious than second, they were going to the milky way and back, they may even frequent the man from Mars whilst on their crusade. Her sordid fingers wrenched his collar, wreathing around his fretful anxiety. He was wearing a rather shapeless turtleneck, an unusual piece of erotical clothing - if I may say so myself. He crossed his fingers, and hoped not to die. Oh, but why?

The grotesque enchantress arrested her fellow through smitten illusionment, issuing his limbs to lax, his lips to slacken, and his eyes to widen. It was errant love at primal sight. She let her soft palette, once more, excrete a pagan sound which profaned a melodious fornication,"Oh, come here, you flirt!"

I ought to add that he was being quite the aphrodisiac. His posture was titillating, his composure was ruttish, and his heart was lewd from lust hagrided. His mind was persuaded she was the one he was to betroth. To be frank, he had little say on that matter. Her clasp dragged him like a coquettish crocodile down to Jigoku. Both are reputed to have been gaily wed.

Thus, we can conclude this chapter by corroborating this fiction as evidence that he lived dolorously ever after.

Epilogue

These harrowing tales are here to highlight the lives we all take for granted. We, the philosophers of our perdurable, meandrous narratives, neglect the smaller things. We commit acts of indecency, commit crimes of inhumanity, and have strayed from the Garden of Eden. It only may be east of our fair land, but alas, we shall never reach it, for we are a shunned race. No other species understands, or has wrought its own moral compass through a manual of scrupulous laws; the irony being that we revoke them by purging these barriers and transgressing them. What is law and order if we abhor the confines of abiding by them? We are puppets to our own harrowing tales. Vices, perversions, bigotries, malices—not a single soul has never not perpetrated one of these acts. No one is perfect; that would be bewildering, nonetheless, we disguise ourselves around a utopian society.

Societal views are, in the main, a load of horse manure. Rules are here chiefly for a tyrannous purpose, however - and here effectuates our paradox - sans them, humans would cannibalise their comrades. We decimate paradisiacal landscapes; we deracinate other ethnicities. We are so ambiguated by our inward connatural prejudice that we concur with discrimination. We neglect the fundamentals of being extent. We are a race that, to prevail, must strike down our opponents with an iron superiority. How does one louse themselves of such loathly contagion? Err anew, by voiding the unbodied gauze that weaves us together? Purging the speculative "inferiors" by means of deluging them, and the "superiors" embark upon Noah's ark? Preposterous! These are insoluble qualms, and shall remain thus for aye.

A reckless troubadour once wrote of Death making angels of us all. Then what does Life make of us?

Hark! and gather round my brethren and sistren: before you next upbraid someone's behaviour, look upon your actions, and introspect ere deflecting your rue upon another. Have you committed a deadly sin? Broken a commandment? or simply even defied the law of our land? He who can admit to his wrongdoings is a man who has accepted the reality of his existence.

"To be ashamed of one's morality: that is a step on the ladder, at the end of which one is also ashamed of one's morality." Good and Evil lie within us all; a true gallant can merge the two to put his own inherent subliminal injustices at bay.

Society will never be cleansed, in a sense, nor should it. For the mere notion of "cleanse" quivers a horrid angst down the spine. We can essay, with ardour, to redress our inequitable infamies, nevertheless, we have arrived at a new terminal in humanity. We, needful fosterlings, now rely on technological advancements to aid us in quotidian life. We distance ourselves further and further from our Mother - our wild Creator. We invent things to do everything for us; no other species gloats in its own indolence. Call me a bore, even a whore, I beseech you to go as far as to say it is ignorance at my core, but I am no swinger, nor am I a dead ringer, I am no puppet, nor am I the puppeteer. We, humans, as nihilistic and pessimistic as I may blither to be, are on a calamitous trajectory, our evolution has been cumbered by a stagnation.

Regardless, I shall conclude this frolicsome ramble here. I fear my contradictions, and misanthropic tropes, abound as illimitable; though I wish to illuminate these gravelling enigmas. Fruit for thought, as they say.

Farewell, my children, until we meet again - adieu!